Beauty and the Books

Book 4 in the Largo Bay Series

Pat Adeff

Apollo Burps Productions

Copyright © 2023 by Pat Adeff

All rights reserved.

No portion of this book may be reproduced in any form without written permission from the publisher or author, except as permitted by U.S. copyright law.

This novel is a work of fiction. References to historical events, real people, or real locales are used fictitiously.

Names, characters, places, and incidents are the product of the author's imagination.

Any resemblance to actual events or locales or persons, living or dead, is purely coincidental.

Contents

1. Chapter One — 1
2. Chapter Two — 7
3. Chapter Three — 11
4. Chapter Four — 17
5. Chapter Five — 23
6. Chapter Six — 29
7. Chapter Seven — 33
8. Chapter Eight — 39
9. Chapter Nine — 43
10. Chapter Ten — 47
11. Chapter Eleven — 53
12. Chapter Twelve — 59
13. Chapter Thirteen — 63

14.	Chapter Fourteen	67
15.	Chapter Fifteen	73
16.	Chapter Sixteen	79
17.	Chapter Seventeen	85
18.	Chapter Eighteen	91
19.	Chapter Nineteen	95
20.	Chapter Twenty	99
21.	Chapter Twenty-One	105
22.	Chapter Twenty-Two	109
23.	Chapter Twenty-Three	115
24.	Chapter Twenty-Four	119
25.	Chapter Twenty-Five	127
26.	Chapter Twenty-Six	133
27.	Chapter Twenty-Seven	137
28.	Chapter Twenty-Eight	143
29.	Chapter Twenty-Nine	149
30.	Chapter Thirty	153
31.	Chapter Thirty-One	161
32.	Chapter Thirty-Two	167
33.	Chapter Thirty-Three	175
34.	Chapter Thirty-Four Four Months Later	183

35.	Author Request	192
36.	Sneak Peek!	193
	Finding Forever: Book 5 in the Largo Bay Series	
37.	Also by Pat Adeff	199

Chapter One

Wren had gotten a good night's sleep – for once. When she finally got up, she actually felt refreshed, which was not her typical way of starting the day. Her normal morning routine usually included at least two cups of coffee just to pry her eyes open.

However last night her son, Caleb, had spent the night at a friend's house, so she took the time to deep clean the kitchen, pay some of their bills, and be in bed before midnight. She even squeezed in thirty minutes of reading before the book fell on her face, letting her know she'd now be able to fall asleep.

It was a luxury she was grateful for.

She was also thankful Caleb had made friends at his new school. In fact, his best friend, Wylie, was just like him; also full of energy and curious about everything. So, Wren had no doubts about if Wylie's mom and dad would be able to handle a child of Caleb's liveliness. In return, next Friday night, Wylie would be Caleb's guest for a sleep over.

She had three hours before Wylie's folks dropped off her son back at the apartment, so Wren figured this might be a good morning to get some long-overdue mending done on their clothes.

Caleb was sprouting up so fast, she couldn't seem to keep up with the way he was outgrowing everything, especially on their limited budget. So, she'd stop by the local church's thrift shop, pick up several pants and shirts for him and then mend anything that needed mending before giving them to him.

He always seemed happy with the outfits she got for him, so things were working out just fine, so far. She was dreading the day he decided he wanted some sort of brand name something-or-other.

She got dressed and made herself a pot of coffee. She poured the heavenly brew into her favorite cup, added heavy whipping cream, and set the cup on the kitchen table.

Then she retrieved the plastic laundry basket from her closet where the need-to-be-mended items awaited her attention. Next, Wren retrieved the sewing kit she kept in the hall coat closet.

She'd just picked out the first item in order to replace a missing button when there was a knock at her front door. She paused before setting aside the garment. She wasn't expecting them back so soon. She squelched down a sigh and went over to look through the peep hole.

Wren inhaled and started to smile.

It was Dom McGannon. And he looked good ... very good – as usual.

She opened the door and was instantly handed a bouquet of flowers obviously from someone's garden. Hopefully from his own was Wren's next quick thought. It made her smile; he didn't just stop by somewhere and pay for a generic bouquet. He'd picked the flowers himself. For her. That meant so much more to her.

"Good morning and thank you!" Her smile made Dom's heart speed up a little bit.

"Good morning and you're welcome."

They stood in the doorway smiling at each other until Dom asked, "May I come in?"

Wren realized she'd been staring into his eyes and quickly backed away from the door to allow him entrance.

"Caleb isn't here this morning. He spent the night at Wylie's house again."

Dom stepped inside and shut the door behind him.

"You should have called me! We could have gone out for dinner somewhere."

When her smile faltered, Dom became uncertain and asked, "Wouldn't you like to go to dinner with me?"

"Oh, sure! Caleb and I had a wonderful time last week. And thank you again for the movie."

"Wren, it was my pleasure."

When her smile still hadn't returned, Dom added. "You do realize that was our first date, right?"

He'd been trying to move slowly with her since she'd made it very clear she had a son and he would always come first. But Dom was ready to make their relationship something steady. He wanted to be someone Wren could depend upon. Plus, he really enjoyed the kid; they got along great.

"No, Dom. It wasn't a date. It was a very nice afternoon outing with you, Caleb, and me."

Dom smiled when he heard that prissy librarian voice come out of her.

"What's so funny?" Wren wasn't sure what he was smiling about, and it made her even more nervous.

"It's nothing funny, Wren." Dom added, "It's just the way you keep trying to hold me at arm's length." He stepped a little closer. "You know I'm interested in you, right?"

Wren's mouth went dry.

What was there about the man that made her feel all feminine and desired? She loved the feeling, but she knew she couldn't have a man in her life right now. Not while she was raising Caleb. In the last town they lived in, she'd been the brunt of several vicious pieces of gossip that weren't true. The fact none of it was true didn't stop the busybodies from spreading the lies, which caused an uncomfortable situation to come about for not only herself, but also for her young son.

She was determined not to have that happen again.

"Look. I know you and Caleb get along great, but I think it might be a good idea for you to not come around so often." She paused before continuing. "I think he's getting attached to you."

"Well, thank goodness one of you is!" Dom shot her a wink and headed into the kitchen where he poured himself a cup of the freshly brewed beverage.

Wren just stood there next to the front door, holding the flowers, watching him move around the kitchen as though he lived there, and not knowing how to handle this.

Yes, she was definitely attracted to him, and he was a really nice guy, and her kid really liked him a lot. But – and there was always a 'but' – he was not what she needed in her life right at the moment.

That said, it wasn't like she could ask, *Dom? Would you please wait until Caleb graduates from high school before you ask me out?* With his looks and his charm, there was no way Dom would wait for her.

She finally got into motion and moved from the doorway into her kitchen. She grabbed a vase from one of the bottom cupboards and filled it with water. After arranging the bouquet, she placed the colorful arrangement on the kitchen's windowsill where the sunlight made the flowers almost glow with their assorted colors.

Dom was sitting in the other chair at the table, enjoying his coffee and watching what she was doing.

"Are you sewing something?" He indicated the pile of clothes and actually sounded interested.

"No. Just some mending."

Wren sat back down, very aware of his closeness, and picked up the shirt again. As she attached the new button, she looked up to find him staring at her. The intensity of his look was somewhat unsettling, so she glanced back down at the shirt in her hands.

Finally, she couldn't handle his unwavering attention or the silence that had engulfed them. "Why are you here, Dom?"

He set down his cup and leaned toward her, again catching her eyes with his.

"I'm here to see what I need to do to get you to agree to date me."

It was as though she was mesmerized by his gaze. She couldn't move and couldn't think of what to say for an answer. She found she was unable to do much of anything except stare right back at him.

Okay, maybe this morning was not going to be the calm morning she'd envisioned for herself.

Chapter Two

Dom thought he did pretty good. He'd gotten Wren to agree to allow him to take her out. Her only addition was that Caleb went with them.

That wasn't a problem for Dom, but he would have to figure out a way he and Wren could be alone together at some point.

He knew Wren was using Caleb as a shield against having to actually agree to a full-on real date, with the potential of romance.

However, the bigger question was what was she going to do when she found out what the fire inspection report contained? He'd been able to get the inspector to hold off for the weekend before letting Wren know what needed to be done.

Such as close the library for a couple of weeks, and probably spend around ten thousand dollars at the least to pay for the repairs.

Since Wren had been hired, she'd been promoted from *library employee* to *assistant librarian*, and was currently holding the position of *head librarian* while Mrs. Turner was on a much-earned four-week vacation.

Mrs. Turner had a new great grandbaby she wanted to see. Now that she felt she had a competent person to run the library while she was gone, she was happy to take the time off and visit her daughter out in Montana.

Unfortunately for Wren, the fire inspection occurred on the second day of Mrs. Turner's vacation. Now, no one will admit it out loud, but none of the guys at the fire department who were qualified to do the inspection really wanted to have to wrangle with Mrs. Turner. The woman was known for her ability to make a grown man instantly feel like they were back in third grade and standing in front of a principal for some infraction. And she did it with just one look.

Nope, no one would ever admit it.

But this gave Dom the problem of putting this on Wren's shoulders. He knew she was barely scraping by financially, herself; her salary wasn't that big. And he bet the library didn't have enough money to cover the repairs. The city council had already passed the budget for the library by the time the fire department got around to its inspection of the dated property.

He'd just have to figure out a way to help her.

Paul stood there, admiring the woman he was going to marry.

Erin had come through the emergency hospital visit in much better condition than he thought she would. In fact, it was kind of a wake-up call for her. She'd seen her doctor the next day and he'd run some more tests. Before putting her on any drugs, he wanted to try to see if she could handle the situation with a change in diet and lifestyle.

Erin certainly didn't want to take medication for the rest of her life, so she decided to use this difficulty as the impetus to change her routine.

And Paul couldn't be happier.

She was in *The Casablanca*'s kitchen prepping for the upcoming dinner crowd. She even looked better rested. One of the changes she made was to drink more water. Oh sure, she thought she was drinking enough, but after saying out loud to her doctor just how much coffee (not actual water) she was consuming, she could see what he was saying. He wasn't going to try to get her to cut down on the caffeine; he just wanted her to increase the amount of plain old water she drank every day.

Another change Erin made was to get herself to bed on time. And that didn't mean "heading for bed" at eleven o'clock. Nope, it meant IN bed by eleven. That, in and of itself, added a full hour of sleep. Now she was getting a full eight hours per night. She'd found that she'd been running on a sleep deficit for years now, without realizing the toll it was taking on her physical health.

These were two slight changes that were making a significant improvement in her day-to-day activities. She was no longer tired all the time. She could focus better. Plus, she wasn't dragging by the end of the day, which was her and Paul's personal time together.

True, they worked together all day and evening, but that was work. It wasn't private time, which is what they realized they needed.

Erin glanced up and saw Paul leaning in the doorway with a smile on his face. Spotting him, she turned over the rest of the prep work to her sous chef (another change she was really trying to make – letting go of some of her kitchen work to others who could do it just as well) and grabbed a towel, wiping off her hands while she walked over to where he was standing.

"Hi there, Handsome." Erin greeted him with a grin and a kiss.

This was another thing Paul enjoyed about the changes she was making. She seemed to be a bit more affectionate now that she wasn't tired all the time. He was so glad she made the changes for her health; he loved her so much and wanted her to be around a very long time. He could picture them together for decades to come, and that picture made his heart swell with the sweetness of it.

"Hi there, yourself!" He wrapped his arms around her and pulled her up against him. She felt so good.

Erin sighed in absolute pleasure.

"You know what?" She whispered in his ear.

"What?"

"We need to do this more often."

"If you're looking for an argument, you're going to have to pick a different subject." His voice was husky with the overwhelming urge he had to kiss her, ardently. It was too bad they were in the middle of a busy restaurant with employees zipping in and out all over the place.

"So, what are you doing after work tonight?" He kissed the tip of her nose instead.

"I thought I'd go for a walk on the beach with my favorite guy."

"Sounds like a good plan."

Chapter Three

"All rise!"

The deep voice of the bailiff was subdued this morning. Usually, he called out loudly with a ring of authority as the judge entered the courtroom. But not this morning. Char glanced over at Bobby to see if he knew what was going on.

He gave his head a small shake. No, he didn't.

The judge slowly ascended the steps and took his seat without looking at anyone, which was what he usually did. Today was definitely different.

Char looked around at the faces of the court clerk, the bailiff, and the stenographer. None of them looked happy.

She glanced over at Bobby again, but he didn't return her look.

He was sitting very still, as though waiting for something to happen.

The judge still hadn't spoken.

She could hear the people sitting in the public area starting to get restless. Each creak of a bench sounded almost too loud.

Someone cleared their throat and it echoed throughout the courtroom.

The time was stretching out much more than it should have.

Char could feel a nervous giggle starting to gather in her throat and tamped it down vigorously. This was no time to allow her nerves to take over!

She could feel Bobby's attention on her but wasn't willing to make eye contact at the moment. She knew if she did, some reaction would come out of her that was not going to help anything.

Finally, the judge looked up.

Char was surprised to see him send a heated glare at Bobby. What the heck!

Bobby didn't seem to react at all; as though he'd been waiting for it.

Then the judge's eyes shifted over to Char.

Well! She had **not** been ready for his piercing scowl. She inhaled sharply before finally being able to snap her mouth closed.

As if satisfied with her reaction, the judge shifted his attention to the people sitting in the public area and finally spoke.

"Ladies and Gentlemen." He stopped a moment before continuing, as though he was still deciding whether to speak or not.

He finally lifted his eyes from his desk. "Ladies and Gentlemen. I have an unfortunate announcement."

Again, he waited, and the wooden benches continued to creak as people shifted, either from boredom or discomfort.

"Due to some unexpected circumstances, I will be taking some personal time away from the courtroom."

It was starting to dawn on Char that Bobby might have moved ahead with his plans to handle the judge and maybe even his boss, the district attorney. She looked over at him, but again he wouldn't look back at her. He just continued to keep his eyes focused on the judge.

The judge continued, "Unfortunately, the cases I was to hear today have been reassigned to other courts. If you would be so kind as to remain in your seats, the court clerk will let each of you know where to report."

He continued to sit there, unmoving, just staring out at nothing, as though he was in shock. The courtroom was absolutely still. No one moved. No one spoke. There wasn't even a creak from the benches.

Finally, without any other words, he stood up and proceeded to go down the steps and exit through the side door.

The bailiff had not announced "All rise" as he normally would have. Instead, he turned toward the crowd who were still sitting silently and addressed them. "You will be handled alphabetically. The court clerk will call out your name. When she does, please step forward. You may come through the half-door and approach her desk. Are there any questions?"

No one seemed to have any, so he walked over to Bobby's desk first and leaned down to speak with him. His voice was so low, Char couldn't hear what they were saying. Bobby listened and then nodded. When he started packing up his briefcase to leave, the bailiff walked over to Char's table.

He leaned down and spoke softly.

"Ms. McGannon, you will be notified when and where your next court dates are. In the meantime, you are welcome to leave." He wasn't friendly, but at the same time, he didn't sound like anything other than tired.

"Thank you, Frank." She had tons of questions but knew this wasn't the time or the place. So, she packed up her papers and left the courtroom.

As she exited through the back double doors, she became aware of how quiet even the rest of the building seemed.

It was almost surreal.

There seemed to be a lack of people, almost like a scene in some movie. There were a handful of folks heading somewhere, but they did not make eye contact and seemed to Char as though they were moving slower than usual.

Or maybe it was her. Char realized she was a little bit in shock with what had just happened.

Now, all she wanted to do was go find Bobby.

She set down her briefcase on one of the empty benches that lined the hallways of the courthouse. Pulling out her phone, she sat down and texted Bobby.

Where are you?

She waited a little bit, but there was no answering text.

Char knew he'd get back to her as soon as he could, so she grabbed her briefcase and headed over to her office.

There was no way Bobby was going to be able to get back with Char that day. He'd be lucky if they could touch base even tomorrow.

He wasn't totally surprised when the judge made his announcement. Bobby had spent the last week in conversations and exchanging emails with one of the investigators at the Florida Judicial Qualifications Division up in Tallahassee. He really hoped he wouldn't be asked to go to their offices, so he'd made sure he checked his phone and email frequently so as to not miss answering their questions in a timely manner.

Now, how to let Char know it would be several days before he could see her again. The problem was that the investigator asked Bobby not to say anything to anyone until he'd finished interviewing everyone on his list.

So how was Bobby supposed to tell Charlie ... what? Nothing?

Chapter Four

Wren knew it wasn't a good idea to be going out tonight with Dom. He'd arranged for all of them to go miniature golfing.

It wasn't that she didn't like miniature golf.

It wasn't that Caleb had never been before, and she knew he'd just love it.

No, it was because she was feeling the jitters about spending more time with Dom. It seemed that no matter how hard she tried, she found herself looking more and more forward to being around him.

She absolutely loved the way he interacted with Caleb. In fact, watching them together told Wren that maybe she'd made a mistake by not allowing any guy into their lives before. Or maybe it was just Dom. There was certainly something about him that just made her days brighter.

She didn't want to feel an attraction to him, but she couldn't seem to stop it from happening.

And now she found herself spending way too much time deciding on what to wear, how to fix her hair, and if she should add a little more eye makeup than usual.

Yep. Jitters.

"Mom!!" Caleb's shout came flying down the hall to Wren's bedroom. "Dom is here! Hurry up!"

Wren smiled at the excitement in her son's voice. She understood the feeling.

She could hear the two of them in the living room as Caleb showed Dom the newest creation he'd made. It was a farming village he was making out of the set of modeling clay Dom had given him as a gift.

At first, Wren had been filled with apprehension at the mess she was just sure Caleb was going to make.

She started to relax when Dom didn't let him open the package until he'd explained to Caleb how to put down one of the plastic sheets he'd also brought. Dom calmly explained how the clay could possibly cause a huge mess if he wasn't paying attention when he worked with the material.

The thing that astonished Wren was the fact Caleb was listening! In fact, he was almost standing at attention and had a solemn look on his face, showing that he understood what Dom was saying and what he was supposed to do.

And, sure enough, Caleb followed Dom's instructions and there had only been one mishap since he started the project last week. A piece of clay had rolled off the table, which would have been fine, since it landed on the plastic Caleb had meticulously put down before he started working. It went off the rails when

Wren had called him from the kitchen for a snack and he'd jumped down off his chair, landed on the bit of clay, and proceeded to tract it into the kitchen.

When Wren had looked down at the path her son had just crossed, her face must have shown her dismay. Caleb immediately looked down at where his mom was looking and realized what he'd just done.

Before Dom had entered their lives, Caleb would have gotten sulky instead of admitting what he'd done. Then there would be several hours of discomfort for both mother and son as she tried to make him fix whatever he'd just caused.

However, this time he looked back up at Wren and announced, "Don't worry, Mom! I know what to do."

And sure enough, he did! Dom had also left a small bottle of natural solvent with a rag. Caleb methodically went about picking up the small pieces of clay that had left a trail from the table into the kitchen. He made sure there was no more clay on the bottom of his shoe. And then he used the solvent and rag to handle the remaining fragments.

You could have bowled Wren over with a slight breeze.

She didn't want to admit that she liked the way her son was becoming calmer when he handled things that hadn't gone his way. Maybe she'd been treating him a little too gently. Whereas Wren would have reacted and then would have tried to make everything okay, Dom just patiently explained things to Caleb as though he assumed Caleb would be able to do what he'd just shown him. It was as though he expected no problems and therefore there weren't any.

Wren figured she could use a little more of that in her life.

Just then, Wren was pulled from her musings.

"MOM!" This time Caleb's voice was showing some impatience with her apparently too-slow pace.

As she was about to answer, she heard Dom call out.

"Yeah, MOM!" She could hear laughter tingeing his voice. And that made her smile.

She did a final check in the mirror and thought she looked pretty good!

When she entered the living room, she could tell from Dom's expression that he thought so too.

What a nice feeling; this appreciation from a handsome man. It was a rare thing for Wren to feel, and she basked in it.

Even Caleb noticed the change in his mom. He wasn't exactly sure what it was, but he could feel her happiness and that made him happy.

Wren headed directly for the front door, purse in hand, calling out, "Come on you slowpokes! What's taking so long?"

Caleb and Dom's laughter followed her out the door as they caught up with her after Dom locked the door behind him.

Caleb had just gotten a hole in one and was jumping around, pumping his fists up into the air. He swung around, still holding the golf club, and just missed hitting Wren in the side. However, as usual, Dom just reached out and caught it without missing a beat.

"Good job, Caleb! That was a great shot!" Wren had missed the near-hit incident and was just extremely happy seeing her son doing so well.

Caleb recognized what he'd almost done and glanced over at Dom to see his reaction.

Dom wiped his forehead as though saying, *that was a near miss*! He smiled as he did it so Caleb wouldn't think he was in trouble.

Then, both of them laughed when they realized that Wren was oblivious to what had almost just happened.

"What's so funny?" Wren was laughing along with them but didn't know what they were laughing about.

Dom reached out and rested his hand on the back of her neck for a moment. "We're just having a really great time; aren't we Caleb?"

"Yep. A really great time." Caleb took back his club when Dom handed it to him. "I'm hungry! Can we get some food?"

Wren couldn't answer. The feel of Dom's warm hand had sent an electrical charge through her that almost made her heart stop. She knew for sure she couldn't concentrate enough to say anything even remotely coherent.

But apparently, she didn't have to speak at all.

"Sure Caleb! What do you say to the Burger Shack?"

"Can I have a chocolate shake, too?"

"Wren?" Dom rubbed her neck gently with his thumb. Her soft skin felt so good to him. He didn't want to stop touching her. Especially since she wasn't pulling away.

"Hmmm?" That was pretty much all Wren was able to mutter. Butterflies had taken residence in her stomach and there was almost an overload of sensations flooding through her.

Dom watched as her face flushed and her breathing changed. He hoped she was responding to his touch. Because he knew he certainly was.

"Burger Shack?" Dom reluctantly released the physical connection between them and started to gather up the golfing equipment.

"Burger Shack?" Wren felt like she was speaking a completely foreign language. It was as though she couldn't recognize words.

"Dinner, Mom!" Caleb tied his shoe after Dom pointed to the lace dragging on the ground. "I'm hungry! Can we go get some dinner? Pleeeeze??"

The yearning expression on her son's face made her chuckle.

"Yes, let's get some dinner." Wren finally made eye contact with Dom and saw the warmth and understanding of what had just occurred between them.

The rest of the evening was spent with the two adults listening and laughing at Caleb's stories about the things he found funny about recess.

Chapter Five

Max walked up to the front of the newest small business to open in Largo Bay. The sign over the front door stated, MARLENE'S MERCANTILE MARKET, which to Max indicated it could contain any sort of merchandise. Furniture? Clothing? A mishmash of garage sale items?

He looked at the display in the front window and still wasn't certain just what it was that Marlene (if there actually **was** anyone by that name) sold. There were pillows, books, wreaths, candles, an old wooden packing crate, an inkwell with pen, some ribbons, what looked to be a handknitted sweater, and a pair of fisherman's rubber boots.

Nope. Not a clue.

When he opened the door and stepped inside he was greeted by the tinkling of an old fashioned doorbell that hung from above the door. The sound made him smile. He closed the door behind him and moved toward one of the packed shelves that lined the wall to the left of him.

The next thing he noticed was a softly perfumed scent that instantly reminded him of Luz. That made his smile fade.

Today started off as one of the days where he missed her desperately. He'd made the decision that getting out and doing a meet-n-greet with people would help.

But no. This just made it worse. It felt like his lungs had frozen and he couldn't draw a breath.

He was about to turn toward the door when a woman called out from the back of the store.

"I'll be right there!"

Marlene stepped out from behind the counter and spotted Max standing there, stock still as though he was a mannequin.

She walked toward him with a smile on her face. He was the first customer to come into her new store since the door opened that morning and she really wanted to meet the people of this new town she'd moved to.

Holding out her hand, she said, "Hello! I'm Marlene. It's nice to meet you."

When Max didn't respond, she kept the smile on her face and added, "Thank you for coming in!"

He seemed to come out of the stupor he'd been in and looked down at her hand then back up to her face. Finally, he reached out and shook the offered hand, closing his mouth and adding a small smile to his face.

"Hello." Even to himself his voice sounded rusty and he had to clear his throat afterwards.

Marlene's first thought had been that the man was someone's grandfather who suffered from dementia and had somehow gotten out of the house. But her opinion quickly changed when his large hand encompassed hers and light came back into his face. No, this man had all his wits about him. He'd probably just been lost in thought.

Max continued, "Welcome to Largo Bay, Marlene, was it?"

She released her hand from his and nodded. "Yes. And this is my new store!" She turned around and held out both arms, indicating the space and everything packed into it. Then she turned back to Max and asked, "Is there something in particular you're looking for?"

Max smiled and shook his head. "No. I'm Max McGannon, the chief of police for Largo Bay."

The smile faded from Marlene's face. "Is there a problem, Sir?"

"Oh, no!" Max was quick to assure the young woman. "Not at all."

He looked around the store, smiling when he spotted what appeared to be a life-size ceramic goose surrounded by several small goslings arranged on top of an old fashion wardrobe steamer trunk.

"I'm here to welcome you to Largo Bay."

"Oh!" Marlene paused for a moment to gather in what the man had just said. Usually when a police officer had showed up at her previous place of employment, it meant trouble. Which is why she left without any forwarding address. She knew she wouldn't receive her last paycheck, but it was worth it to disappear.

However, apparently having a police officer show up meant something entirely different in Largo Bay!

Nice! Marlene knew she was going to like living here. Especially because she was certain neither Ben nor his family could find her. She'd left absolutely no clues as to where she'd gone. Maybe she'd be able to breathe freely now.

"That's very nice of you, Sir." Marlene gave him a smile of relief.

"Please, call me Max. *Sir* makes me feel old." Max smiled back. He'd noticed the look of panic cross her face earlier and wondered where it had come from. Maybe he'd find out later.

Marlene gave him a full tour of her shop, explaining occasionally where she'd found one of the treasures she had on display.

"How do you decide what to put in your shop?" Max was curious about the young woman and if she even had a business plan of any sort. Did people really buy these sorts of things? At least enough for her to make a living?

"It speaks to me." Marlene had her back to Max when she answered his question and missed the look of disbelief he gave her.

"It speaks to you?" Max's skepticism came through his question.

She turned to face him before answering.

She'd run into other people before who doubted her ability to stock a store with sellable merchandise; Ben for one. And now this nice man was questioning how she did it. But this time she wanted to explain it so it didn't sound weird or oddly hocus-pocus-y. She wanted to fit in with this new town.

"When I spot an item at a yard sale or antique store, I have already researched enough to know if there is a market for it or not."

Max reconsidered his previous worry about a business plan. Even if she didn't have anything in writing, she appeared to know her market.

She watched as the doubt regarding her business abilities left Max. He smiled before answering, "I had no idea there was a market for gee-jaws like what you're selling here." He rubbed the back of his head before adding, "But I'm glad there is!"

"Me, too!"

Max arrived home with his daughter's birthday gift. He was still amazed he'd paid seventy-five dollars for the tiny, gilded hand mirror he'd gotten Shea. He shook his head at himself. He'd never seen her even glance in the mirror at the station, much less spend any amount of time looking at herself in a bejeweled handheld device. Maybe he'd made a mistake. But no. Marlene had assured him she would love it.

He guessed only time would tell and he'd either be the best dad when it came to presents or a complete imbecile when it came to what young women actually wanted. He surprised himself when he realized he hadn't had Luz swamp his thoughts while he was in the store, after he'd gotten over the scent.

In fact, he'd felt kinda good.

Marlene was straightening up one of the shelves, thinking about how Max had purchased the gift for his daughter in spite of his reservations. She knew it would be a great gift. And she knew he'd relied on her expertise to make his decision to go ahead a buy it.

That made her feel pretty good to have someone trust her intuition on what would be a great gift for one of their children.

She wondered if his wife usually bought the gifts for friends and family. And if she did, why wasn't she purchasing this one?

Chapter Six

Zach had to nudge Luca again.

"Dude! Did you hear me?"

Luca turned wide disbelieving eyes at him. "I'm not sure I did. Please repeat it."

The grin that split Zach's face said it all.

"Your song, *Bella*, made the top one hundred music chart this week. And it's only been out several days!"

"That's because of all your managing, social media posts, and sending it to everyone at any station you could get an email address for!" Luca hugged his friend. "Dude! You made it happen!"

"Yeah, but I couldn't have done it without your song." Zach couldn't stop grinning, either. "It's one of the best songs I've ever heard."

"Thanks. I had a great muse for it!"

"How's Shea doing with you being gone right now?"

"It's hard to tell. She tries to keep it to herself, but I know it still bothers her." Luca ran a hand through his hair. "I wish I could figure out a way we could be together all the time."

"Yeah. I hear you." Zach wished that could happen, too. He didn't like seeing Luca worrying about his girlfriend. He knew it really bothered his friend.

"So, how long is Luca gone for this time?" Erin was just putting the finishing touches on a cake that she'd made for Shea's birthday party which was happening in a couple of days.

The sisters were in the kitchen at *The Casablanca* restaurant. It was that lull time between the lunch rush and the dinner crowd. Shea had stopped by to get a sandwich for her late lunch and was sitting at the two-seater table in the kitchen area, usually reserved for family and friends.

Shea took another bite from her sandwich, chewed it, and tried to swallow, but her dry throat wouldn't allow the bite to move. So, she ended up taking a large drink of her iced tea and forced the food down.

After she was sure the food had successfully made the trip to her stomach, Shea shrugged as though it didn't matter to her about Luca being gone. "We're not sure. Apparently, his new song is doing pretty well, so he might be gone a little while longer than we originally thought."

Erin didn't buy her sister's nonchalant attitude one bit. She set down the cake knife and went over to join her at the table.

"Shea. You can tell me." She reached over and took Shea's hands in her own. "I know you don't like it when Luca's gone. Please talk to me. Let me help."

Shea hated the fact she couldn't seem to handle her reaction whenever Luca left. It wasn't that she didn't trust him. She trusted him completely. It wasn't that she thought he'd never come back. She knew that wouldn't happen.

It was just something that she couldn't put her finger on, except that when the unpleasant emotions rolled on in, it made her miserable and she didn't know how to stop it.

She let out a sigh and looked directly at Erin.

"I feel like such a baby when I do this!" And then to both her and Erin's surprise, she started to cry.

Luca and Zach were heading into the city to meet up with the producer of Luca's new album.

The drive down the Hudson was breathtaking. With autumn in the air, the leaves were starting to turn and the various shades of orange, russet, and red lined both sides of the wide river. Luca wished Shea was there with him. He just knew she'd love the fall season in New York. Maybe she could fly up for the weekend!

This weekend! Oh no. It was Shea's birthday this weekend. Her family was having a huge get together at Max's house. When Luca had left Largo Bay last week, he'd figured he'd be home on Friday. But it didn't look like that was going to happen.

This was not good.

"Hey, Zach. Is there any way we can possibly postpone Saturday's meeting? I totally forgot this weekend was Shea's birthday and I need to be home for it."

Zach was driving so he wasn't able to check his electronic tablet..

"I'm not sure. When we get to the studio, remind me and I'll check the calendar."

"Okay. Thanks."

Luca turned his head to the window and stared out at the brightly colored leaves again. It was too bad he wasn't actually seeing them.

Chapter Seven

Erin grabbed a handful of tissues from the back countertop and handed the wad to Shea. She couldn't remember the last time she'd seen her sister cry. Usually, Shea just put up a stoic front that their family referred to as her "cop face." They knew she was hurting, but they also knew she didn't want to look like a wimp in front of anyone, so they didn't pursue any questions when she was in cop mode.

However, this time was too much for Erin. She wanted to see her sister happy, but if Shea was going to get like this every time Luca had to leave, it was going to be miserable for Shea and everyone around her.

Something had to change.

Shea mopped her face with the tissues and finally dried her tears. Looking across the table at Erin, she shrugged and gave a self-deprecating half smile.

"I don't know what gets into me. It's just so overwhelming that I can't even think! It's like an avalanche that buries me within seconds. I just seem unable to pull out of it."

Erin leaned across the table. "I know. I get that way sometimes myself."

Shea looked up, stunned at hearing her big sister confess anything like that. She thought Erin had everything under control in her life.

Erin laughed at her sister's reaction. "You think you're the only one who can't control their emotions? The truth is I don't think anyone is very good at it all the time. The only thing I've found that helps me is to focus on the here and now. You know, like where am I? And what's around me. Maybe even just noticing the ground under my feet sometimes helps. I can't guarantee it'll work every time, but it's certainly worth a try. You know?"

"I had no idea you had trouble with that also!" Shea's tears had dried up at Erin's statement. "You always seem to have everything together."

Erin threw her head back as she brayed laughter.

Well, of course, Erin's laughter helped Shea release whatever it was that had taken over for a while, and she joined her sister in the mirth.

The two women sat there laughing. This time good tears came to Shea's eyes as she released some emotion.

Finally, they both calmed down. Feeling much better at this point, Shea reached across the table and took one of Erin's hands in hers.

"Thank you." She squeezed her sister's hand. "I really needed that!"

"I think we both did." Erin squeezed back.

" I need to text Luca back!"

Erin watched as Shea jumped up from the table and headed for the door. She felt good she'd been able to help. Sometimes it just took a friendly, caring ear to make things better.

"See ya!" Erin shouted out as her sister hurried out of the restaurant.

"Love ya!" The response let Erin know Shea was going to be just fine.

Dom was trying to hurry to get to the library before the Fire Captain got there to tell Wren about the fire codes that needed repair. He knew the news would be devastating to her and wanted to be there for her.

He wished now that he hadn't taken the time for his morning's run. He mentally chastised himself that he hadn't thought to check his phone first.

One of Dom's coworkers had texted him to let him know the captain was heading over to the library. The man had gotten word from the city's attorney that morning that he'd legally run out of time and had to present the findings to the librarian today, so the library could be closed and remain closed until the repairs had been done. That way they would be in compliance with Largo Bay's safety codes.

Dom's face fell in dismay when he saw the Chief's truck parked in the fire zone area near the library's front door.

That meant Wren was already being informed about the library's necessity to close. He knew it was not going to go well.

He parked and sprinted into the building just in time to hear Wren's loud protest.

"What?! No. That can't be!"

Hearing the distress in her voice made him grimace as he slowed his speed and approached the front desk where Wren sat most of the time.

"Mrs. Johnson," The Fire Chief started but was cut off by Wren.

"It's Ms. Johnson." Wren had no idea why she felt the need to announce that particular fact. It actually was not relevant to the current discussion.

"Ms. Johnson," He tried again. "We've given you more time than usual before bringing this to your attention."

Wren turned her eyes on Dom. The look on his face said everything. He'd known about this! Even when he'd taken them miniature golfing last weekend, he'd known about this! And hadn't said one word!

"You!" Dom was pinned to the floor by Wren's one-word accusation. He couldn't think. He couldn't do anything other than just stand there next to the Chief while he watched Wren's eyes fill with tears.

"Ms. Johnson," the chief seemed oblivious to Wren's distress with Dom's actions. "I'm afraid we're going to have to close and secure the library for now; until the repairs are made."

Wren's wrath turned back to the captain, "And just how am I supposed to do that? Does the town of Largo Bay have enough money to cover it? Do I have to turn away library patrons starting today? Just what exactly am I supposed to do with your decrees?"

Wren was livid. She couldn't have lowered her voice if she'd tried, which at the moment she did not care one whit about.

The captain was starting to fidget. This was not going the way he'd hoped. He turned to Dom for support.

"Anything you'd like to add?" He had no problem shifting the irate woman's attention back to the younger firefighter.

Dom's look of defeat said it all for both the captain as well as Wren.

"Wren," Dom started to explain his idea for the needed repairs fundraising.

"It's Ms. Johnson to you." Wren's voice was like ice and stopped him dead in his tracks.

Dom glanced over to the captain to see if there was any help available from that direction, only to watch the man pull out the sign that would be posted on the library's front doors.

Dom's heart fell to his feet, knowing he'd made the wrong decision in not telling Wren what was happening. Sure, he'd thought he was protecting her. But it only took one look at her to realize she felt betrayed and hurt.

He just stood there, not knowing what to do next to make this all right.

Chapter Eight

Wren was able – finally – to turn off her phone. She'd already picked up Caleb from school and she didn't need to hear from anyone else.

She didn't **want** to hear from anyone else.

Especially from that awful man, Domenic McGannon!

If she NEVER heard from him again, it would be too soon.

He'd duped her. He'd lied to her. Well, not outright lied, but he hadn't told her what he knew about the library going to be closed. That was just as bad. He purposefully withheld information from her. Important information she needed to know!

"Mom?" Caleb's soft voice interrupted her dark thoughts. He knew something was wrong but didn't understand what it was.

Wren put on her best smile, which was too big and didn't reach her eyes. "Yes, Caleb?"

Caleb had learned over his short number of years just when was the right time to speak and when was not. He figured, correctly, that this was not one of those times. So instead, he asked a safe question, "Can I have some cereal? I'm hungry."

"Of course." Wren relaxed a little when she understood that he wasn't going to ask her what had happened. "You know how to get it, right?" She reached out and ruffled his hair with her fingers, which seemed to make him happy.

She watched her son walk into the kitchen and could hear him opening the cupboard and getting out a bowl. Then she heard the sounds of the kitchen drawer opening and heard the clink of flatware when he retrieved a spoon. The cereal pouring into the bowl made a slight rustling sound.

Wren found herself tightening up a little when Caleb opened the refrigerator door. She really did not want to have to clean up a milk spill right now. She waited to hear the splash of milk on the floor, but it never happened. She heard the milk go into the bowl and then a few seconds later, the refrigerator door closed.

As her muscles relaxed, she made herself move down the hallway to her room. It was time to get out of her work clothes and put on her comfort clothes.

She smiled at the phrase she'd come up with. Instead of comfort food, she used comfort clothes to help make everything right with the world again. That was not to say that comfort food was not part of her life – it was. But right now, all she wanted was to be in her old sweatpants that were too big and her oldest tee shirt that was stretched out and saggy.

And since she was now ensconced at home and it was just family, she wanted complete comfort, so no bra. Slippers completed the outfit.

She grabbed a big scrunchie and pulled her hair back into a ponytail.

Yep, she already felt a little bit better.

She headed back down the hall and entered the kitchen to find Caleb sitting at the kitchen table, reading a book while eating his cereal!

"What are you reading?" Wren was surprised to see him so engrossed in it.

"It's a book Dom said I should read." Caleb didn't look up from it and shoved another spoonful of cereal into his mouth.

Wren felt her whole body tighten back up with irritation. Can't the man ever go away? She's safe in her own home and yet it feels as though he was right there.

She knew was being irrational but couldn't help it. He'd invaded her life and turned everything around to where she didn't know if she could manage or not. Right up until the moment Dom showed up at her doorstep, she'd had everything under control ... pretty much.

Wren knew she needed to calm down. She knew she needed to chill out.

So, she made herself a small pot of coffee.

Just what she needed.

Caffeine to help rev her up even more than she already was.

Whatever, it was soothing to at least make the coffee. It was one of those comforting actions, sort of like folding towels fresh from the dryer on a chilly day. Comforting.

She never did get around to asking Caleb what the book was about.

Dom knew he'd blown it.

Big time!

Now, Wren was never going to go out with him again.

And that thought physically hurt.

For once in his life, he was unwilling to just walk away from a woman. Over the years, he'd gotten really good at ending a relationship, usually on his own terms. He'd remained friends with all the gals, for the most part.

And yet, here Wren had ended the relationship with him. And definitely not on good terms.

He wasn't willing to just let her go. He wasn't willing to walk away from

Caleb either. He'd come to really care about how the kid was going to do in life.

Okay. So how to fix this?

He wasn't sure, but he knew he had to try.

Dom just wasn't ready to no longer have them in his life.

He needed them.

Chapter Nine

"Dom. You knew I couldn't hold off telling her any further." The fire captain was trying to placate the irate man. "The city council's attorney gave me more time than he should have."

Dom let out a breath before replying.

"I know, Chief." He ran a hand through his already messy hair. He'd been trying all morning to come up with some sort of solution for getting the library repairs fully funded and done, so Wren could get back to work.

Although the city was going to pay her while the library was closed, he knew Wren wanted to be working. She needed to be working. He already knew that about her.

"But isn't there something we can do to get the repairs started soon, instead of waiting for some sort of grant to come through?"

"Do you have fifteen thousand dollars to donate?" The Chief was asking a legitimate question.

"Unfortunately, no." Dom wasn't good at saving money and knew he had less than a thousand in the bank. Since he didn't have any huge responsibilities financially, he didn't pay much attention to what he spent. At least, up until now.

The chief could see Dom's concern and offered up another suggestion.

"What about some sort of fundraiser?"

"What kind of fundraiser?" Dom felt maybe there might be a solution after all.

"I'm not an expert, but my wife has helped on several over the years. I know the women's group she's part of raised around twenty thousand last year with their annual silent auction at the country club."

Dom looked hopefully at the man. "How long did it take?"

The chief thought for a moment before he answered. "If I recall correctly, they start the silent auction planning in May." He looked up at Dom. "The event is held is December."

Dom's jaw tightened. "That's too long. We need something to happen right now!"

"Well, I'm sorry, but that's all the advice I can give." The chief stood up, relieved, as the station bells sounded. "Let's get to work."

And both men headed downstairs to go out on the call. Something they were experts at, unlike fundraising.

Luca couldn't wait to see Shea.

He was on a plane heading home to Largo Bay. Unfortunately, he didn't get through to her to let her know he was on the way before the plane attendants asked everyone to turn off their phones and other electronic devices.

Sitting in the seat next to him was Zach.

They'd both decided to take the weekend off for Shea's birthday party on Sunday. And besides, Luca felt that Shea needed to meet Zach, in order to feel better about when he was off on tour.

"We can either put you up at a hotel, or you can sleep at my place. We can pick up some sort of temporary bed for you on the way home." Luca really wished he had a bigger place.

"That's okay. I'm fine with a hotel." Zach turned and grinned at his friend. "Just make sure it has great views of the beach!"

Luca knew he was talking about the view of the women who might be on the beach and laughed.

"Don't worry, there will be plenty of time to meet women."

They both settled back in their seats as the flight attendants pushed the drink cart down the aisle with their usual patter of "watch your elbows."

"Hey, Dad!" Erin was checking in to see if there was anything Max needed for her to pick up for Shea's party.

"Hey, yourself!" Max was always delighted to hear from one of his kids.

"Just wanted to coordinate any last minutes items we might need for Sunday."

"Nope. I think everything's handled. Especially at your end!"

Erin was bringing all the food and the birthday cake, which Max figured was all that really mattered.

"Did you pick up the beverages?" Erin had her checklist on the desk in front of her and was checking everything off.

"Yep. Everything's here and ready to go into a tub full of ice."

"Dad? Would it be okay with you if we used Mom's good dishes?" Erin wasn't sure how Max would feel about unpacking all the plates.

"Honey, I think that's a great idea." Max smiled at his daughter's apparent reticence about asking. "Your mom would love the idea."

"Thank you, Dad!" Erin scratched off the disposable plates from her list. She was also happy about her dad's response. He didn't sound lost this time when he mentioned Luz.

"Paul and I will get there around noon to help set up everything."

"I'm looking forward to it. See you then." Max's cheerfulness came through his voice.

"See you then. Love you." Erin smiled at her dad's response.

"Love you more."

And the call ended.

Shea tried calling Luca, but once again it went directly to voicemail. She knew he didn't check his VM very often, so she didn't bother leaving a message.

She knew her disappointment in not reaching him was a little over the top, but she really wanted to speak with him.

She'd recently been having some doubts about how their relationship was going to be able to work. It wasn't a conscious doubt; more like a feeling that crept up and took unwanted residence in her mind.

Shea put her phone back in her pocket, finished her lunch, and went back to work.

Chapter Ten

The plane finally landed at the Ft. Lauderdale airport and Luca happily turned his phone off airplane mode. After exiting the plane, he and Zach found a close-by coffee shop and grabbed a couple of seats at a small table toward the front of the shop.

Zach placed their orders while Luca called Shea.

"Hi!" Shea sounded tired but glad to hear from him.

"Hi, mi Bella!" Luca felt relief he'd finally reached her. "You'll never guess where I am."

Shea was too tired to guess but didn't want to disappoint him by not even trying. "New York?"

"Not even close."

"England?"

Luca laughed. "I'm a thirty minute car ride from you."

Shea's tiredness left her immediately. "Oh, Luca! Really?"

"Yes. Really. I missed you so much."

"I missed you too."

"You have to make a choice." Luca's statement came out of left field.

"Choice? What do you mean?"

"I can either rent a car or you can come get us at the airport."

Shea grinned. "Of course, I'll come get you!" She paused as she realized he'd said "us."

"Who's 'us'?" She couldn't imagine (and really didn't want to) who might be with Luca.

"I brought Zach with me to meet you! I assume it's okay for him to come to your birthday party."

Immediately, Shea wasn't sure she was ready to meet Luca's new manager. For some reason, if she didn't really know Zach then Luca's career was less threatening to her. After that thought flitted through her mind, she took a deep breath and made the decision to put on her big girl panties and actually stop being such a wimp about the whole thing.

"Of course it is! I can't wait to meet him when I pick you up." Shea was just happy Luca was finally home. "I'll be there soon and will text when I arrive!"

"Can't wait! Oh, by the way, Zach will be staying at my place. Do you happen to have an air mattress of any sort?"

"No. But I do have a guest room."

"Uh, nope. My friend is not going to be staying at your place while I get to go home, alone, to my little apartment.:

Shea laughed.

"I'm sure my dad would be happy to have him stay at the big house. There is more than enough room."

"Wow! That would be awesome!"

"I'll call my dad and get his approval before I come get you guys."

"Thank you!" Luca's voice lowered. "I can't wait to hold you in my arms."

And with that declaration from him, all of Shea's worries dissolved into thin air.

Her own voice was softer. "Bye."

"Bye."

Luca was grinning as he set his phone down on the table.

Zach arrived back at the table with their orders. "Okay. Coffee, black, extra shot of espresso for you. And mocha cinnamon latte with foam for me."

Luca glanced at his friend. He knew he hadn't heard that last part right.

Zach threw his head back and laughed. "Gotcha!"

Yep, Luca was very glad he'd gotten Zach to agree to be his new manager. He had a great sense of humor as well as an outstanding work ethic. He knew he was in the right hands for the next part of his music career.

Luca pretended to look inside Zach's cup then back up at Zach.

"What? No sprinkles?"

They both had a good laugh.

"Hey, Dad! I'm on my way to get Luca and his manager Zach from the airport. Can I ask a huge favor of you? Can Zach stay in one of the extra bedrooms at your place?"

Max liked how the shadows that had been circling around Shea seemed to have disappeared. "Of course, it's alright. There's plenty of room here. Do you know when you'll arrive? I was just heading out to pick up a bite to eat."

"We won't be there for at least another hour. Probably an hour and a half."

"Perfect. See you then, Shea."

"Thanks, Dad. Love you."

"Love you more."

After ending the call, Shea quickly changed her outfit, brushed her teeth, and refreshed her make-up. Heading out the door she felt lighter than she had for some time.

For some reason, the traffic was extra heavy that evening and it took Shea just over an hour to get there.

She spotted the men standing next to their bags in the arrivals area and slowly pulled over closer to them, finally snatching a spot at the curb when a van pulled out of it.

She put the car in park and opened her door to step out where she was immediately engulfed in Luca's warm arms. She sighed as she wrapped her own arms around his waist. He leaned his head down and his mouth captured hers.

This kiss was different than any of the others they'd shared so far.

This kiss was filled with emotion, longing, something that felt just like coming home.

They finally broke apart when someone behind Luca cleared his throat in a definite manner.

"Sorry to interrupt, but the airport security asked me if there was anything I could do to move us along."

The smile across Zach's face showed that he wasn't sorry at all. However, he had been asked and had agreed to see if he could hurry things up.

"Zach, meet Shea." Luca still had an arm around her waist holding her fast to his side. "Mi Bella, meet Zach, the man who runs my music business."

Shea reached out a hand to him, "Great to finally meet you, Zach!"

Zach took her hand in his, but instead of shaking it as she'd intended, he brought it up to his lips and he kissed the back of it before finally letting go when Luca growled at him.

"It is totally my pleasure, Shea. I can see why Luca was anxious to get home to you."

"Okay, Dude." Luca had a pretend scowl on his face. "You can let go of her hand any time now."

Just then, the airport security blew his whistle in their direction, so Shea quickly got in the car while the guys put their bags in the trunk then hopped in, Luca riding passenger with Zach in the back seat.

The ride to Max's was filled with laughter while both Luca and Zach regaled Shea with some stories about one of the producers they'd decided not to sign with. It appeared that the man kept reptiles all over his office, which in and of itself was not the creepy part. It was how he had his receptionist feed the reptiles live crickets and small mice. The joy on the man's face was out of place and had given both Luca and Zach a bad feeling so Zach mentioned they had another appointment and they'd get back to him. It took less than fifteen seconds for them to get out of the office and into the elevator which took them to the first floor.

When they finally got outside, onto the sidewalk, all they could do was laugh at the situation.

Shea enjoyed the way Luca and Zach spoke, one completing the other's sentence. They seemed to be good friends, which made her more comfortable with Zach being Luca's new manager. She knew he'd been burned badly before and wanted to see him succeed this time.

Now to just figure out a way for her to feel better about when he had to leave to go on tour.

Chapter Eleven

Against her better judgment, Wren drove past the library Saturday morning. She'd just dropped off Caleb at Wylie's house for a day trip the family was taking to one of the nearby zoos. Caleb was excited to see the different animals.

She parked at the end of the walkway that led to the front door and frowned when she saw the red notice plastered on it. Yep, it was still there. Some miracle had not occurred and the library had not opened without the repairs having to be done.

Wren wasn't sure how long she sat there, lost in her thoughts. However, she came back to the here and now when someone rapped on her car's window.

Wren inhaled sharply and jerked around to see who was there.

It was Mrs. Abbott, the volunteer woman who came in Saturday mornings and helped straighten up the bookshelves.

Wren groaned when she realized she'd forgotten to call the woman. She rolled down her window so they could speak.

"I'm so sorry Mrs. Abbott. I should have called you yesterday." Wren was anxious about not losing the woman's invaluable help.

"Oh, sweetie. It's okay. I know this must have been quite the shock. Especially while (name of head librarian) is off on her vacation." Mrs. Abbott was not only efficient with the books but was also one of those very kind people who honestly care about others.

Wren blew out a breath. "This has been so hard. I'm not sure how to get the money to make the repairs."

"That shouldn't be too difficult a problem to solve. People here in Largo Bay usually jump in and help when they know there's a need." The older woman paused before gently chastising, "You need to reach out for help. I know you want to handle it all on your own, but dear, there's no reason for that when so many would be willing to help if they only knew."

A blush of embarrassment worked its way up Wren's neck until she could feel the heat infuse her face. "You're right, Mrs. Abbott. I do usually try to handle things myself. I'm afraid it's a habit I've gotten into over the years."

"Well, of course it is! Raising a child as a single mother is a terrific burden. Many women can't do it, but you are one of those rare mothers who do."

Wren waited for her to continue with a comment or two, asking where the father was, etc. But instead, the woman just stood there with her hand gently resting on Wren's arm and a gentle smile on her face.

Then she added, "Unfortunately it takes its toll in difficult ways that no one else could understand unless they had been through it also."

Wren realized she was talking about herself!

Her eyes widened at the realization, and Mrs. Abbott just nodded yes at her.

Suddenly there was a connection between the two women from different generations but similar situations. A friendship was born.

About fifteen minutes later, Wren and Mrs. Abbott were sitting at one of the tables at *It's A Grind* enjoying their soup and half-sandwiches.

Wren had only been to the coffee shop one other time, and that was to get a treat for Caleb. This time, she figured she could afford to get lunch without draining her savings account. The fact was, Wren was very good at saving money. In fact, she could pinch a penny until it screamed for mercy.

She was saving for Caleb's college tuition and books. At the rate she was going putting away the money, she knew she'd have just enough for him to attend a state college, if he continued to live at home. The cost for him to go to a university was outrageous, and she certainly didn't want him strapped with a debt of tens of thousands of dollars before he'd even started his adult life. That was no way for anyone to live.

However, if she cut back on using her car during the time the library was closed, she could certainly pay for one lunch.

Agnes, one of the owners of *It's A Grind* came over to their table with a plate of cookies for the ladies.

When Wren started to protest they hadn't ordered the sweet treats, Agnes set down the plate and put her hands on her hips. The 1940's red polka dot dress was her standard uniform and seemed to fit her style perfectly.

"Young lady, these are samples of our new recipes. In exchange for your opinion of them, there is no charge.

Realizing she'd offended the woman, Wren replied, "And I would love to taste them and give you my opinion. My son just loves your chocolate macadamia nut cookies."

Agnes relaxed her arms and smiled at the young woman as if she'd said the most remarkable thing.

"Your son has excellent taste."

At that, Agnes turned around without even a farewell, humming an Andrew's Sisters song and popping her bubble gum.

Mrs. Abbott and Wren watched the woman head back into the kitchen, then turned to each other and shared a smile of understanding at the woman's behavior, which had turned out to be delightful.

Outside, Dom drove past and noticed Wren's car parked in front of the coffee shop. He hurriedly found the next open parking spot and hightailed it into the place.

He spotted Wren sitting at a table with Mrs. Abbott, one of his favorite people in Largo Bay.

He strode across the room and came to a stop next to their table.

"Why, Dom!" Mrs. Abbott exclaimed. "What a nice surprise." She turned to Wren to introduce her to the young man but stopped when she saw the angry glare Wren was giving Dom.

All of a sudden the air around them felt jammed packed with unspoken waves of something. And it didn't feel like it was full of fun either.

Wren could only stare at him. She hated that he still made her feel something for him. If she could only be angry at him, she'd do just fine. But no, she still had to be attracted to the man, despite his treachery and deceit.

Dom couldn't get enough of looking at Wren even though she looked like she would be more than happy to do him harm.

"Wren, could we please talk?" Dom was finally able to make his mouth form words.

Instead of answering, Wren stood up, gathered her purse, and headed to the ladies room at the back of the coffee shop.

Dom watched her walk away, back stiff and steps fast.

After what seemed like a lifetime, he felt a hand on his arm. It was Mrs. Abbott.

"Dom, that young lady seems a bit miffed with you."

He barked out a single laugh. "You have no idea, Mrs. Abbott. I don't think I've ever had any woman as angry with me as she is." He turned to look at the woman. "And I don't know how to fix it."

"Oh, you poor dear." Mrs. Abbott could feel the exchange of heat passing between the two young people and could certainly spot love when it was right in front of her.

"How about if you stop by my house in about an hour. I'll fix some coffee and bring some goodies from here. I think I can help."

Dom was willing to try anything if only he could get back in Wren's good graces. Heck, he'd settle for being barely tolerated by her at this point.

"Okay, Mrs. A." Dom looked toward the back one more time. "I'll be there." Then he left so Wren wouldn't have to hide all day in the coffee shop's bathroom.

Wren came out after Mrs. Abbott stuck her head in the door and announced, "All clear!"

Not a word was spoken about Dom showing up.

However, the feedback they gave to Agnes was effusive to the point she boxed up more of the delights for them to take with them.

Chapter Twelve

Dom's idea of what "coffee and goodies" meant was much different than what he had imagined Mrs. Abbott would offer.

Not even close.

Mrs. Abbott had a full "high tea" set-up ready when he arrived.

The coffee table in front of her couch was adorned with a silver tea tray, a silver coffee urn, a small cream pitcher, and sugar bowl complete with small silver tongs.

Sitting next to the gorgeous silver array were beautiful fine porcelain cups and saucers.

And next to that was a three-tiered tower covered with not only the goodies from the coffee shop, but also various small triangular sandwiches and tiny pastel colored rectangles, which Dom was instructed by the woman were petite fours.

After sitting in the chair located on the other side of the coffee table, Dom was handed a plate that matched his cup and saucer, upon which she'd provided a couple of sandwiches as well as a selection of the various other sweet items on the tower.

The word uncomfortable did not even begin to describe the way Dom felt. All of a sudden, his hands were too large and clumsy. He thanked her and set the plate down in front of him and waited to see how Mrs. Abbott was going to proceed. He figured with this fancy a layout, there just must be some sort of ritual that came with it.

And sure enough, he was right.

Mrs. Abbott gave him an approving smile when he sat back in his chair and waited.

"How do you take your coffee, young man?" She'd just poured from the urn into one of the cups and held it in the air in front of her, waiting for his answer.

"A little cream, please."

Again, he received a pleased nod of her head.

Okay. So far so good.

She handed him the cup and saucer after adding cream and stirring it without the spoon hitting the sides or bottom of the porcelain cup even once. Dom wasn't sure he'd ever heard complete silence before while a spoon was stirring in a cup. When he was eating in a restaurant, his always clinked and clanked. Impressive.

Dom followed her lead with everything. If she took a bite from one of the small sandwiches, he took a bite, whereas usually he'd just pop the whole thing in his mouth.

When she took a sip of her coffee, he took a sip of his coffee, and this time not smacking his lips in appreciation.

Always earning her approval as though he was being put to some sort of test.

Which it turns out was exactly what she was doing.

"Very good, Domingo." She smiled over the rim of her cup. "You passed."

Dom smiled in relief. "I knew there was a test of some sort, but I couldn't figure it out."

"In fact, you passed with flying colors!" Mrs. Abbott sat back against the back of the couch. "You proved to me you could follow a woman's instructions without having to be told what to do. You were able to pick up on my signals and respond correctly."

Now he was puzzled. How in the heck was that going to help him fix what was wrong between Wren and himself?

"You can go ahead and relax now. Would you rather have a mug for your coffee?" The woman was already up on her feet and heading for the kitchen.

He called after her, "Yes, please!"

She immediately reentered the living room with two mugs in her hands.

He laughed. She must have had them sitting right on the counter waiting for her to retrieve them.

After that, things felt a lot more relaxed. Dom was actually surprised at the amount of food he packed away while listening to her. She certainly made a ton of sense!

Now if he could execute their plan correctly.

It sounded like it should work.

Wren felt exhausted. She was very much enjoying the coffee and baked items at the coffee shop. Right up until the moment HE had to show up and ruin everything.

Well, actually if she was going to be truly honest with herself, it hadn't been all that enjoyable. She'd had to work really hard at not bursting into tears while speaking with Mrs. Abbott.

The woman seemed to truly understand the problem about the library, and her empathy was almost too much for Wren to bear.

In fact, she felt better with her anger at Dom than she did with her feeling of hopelessness discussing how to get the money for the repairs.

She wasn't willing to contact Mrs. Turner because she was finally on vacation probably having the time of her life with the new grandbaby.

And frankly, there just wasn't anyone else to turn to for help.

Wren put her head back down on the couch cushion and fell into a fitful sleep.

Chapter Thirteen

Wren woke up with a headache from the strange position her neck had bent during the nap. She felt disoriented and had the strong feeling she'd forgotten something.

Caleb?! Where was Caleb?

She'd leapt to her feet before remembering he was with Wylie and his family. They wouldn't return until after dark.

She collapsed back down onto the couch and leaned forward, holding her head in her hands. This can't really be happening, can it? She'd only been in charge of the library for a couple of days before it had been officially closed. Talk about being a failure. What was wrong with her anyway? Why couldn't something just go the way it was supposed to for once in her life?

The only bright spot in her current darkness was her son. He was everything to her and she had sworn when he was born that he'd be given every opportunity she'd missed. She also promised that she'd never abandon him, no matter how his life turned out. She'd be there for him whenever he needed her.

Her son was not going to go through what she had suffered through with her parents when she'd gotten pregnant. You would have thought she'd done it on purpose just to cause them personal heartache and grief. When they turned their backs on her for "bringing shame down upon our good family name," she thought she had committed the worst sin in the whole history of the world.

Now, even though she realized it was their problem and not hers, she still carried remnants of the guilt of failing them and everyone else who had been in her life. Including her boyfriend at the time. When he'd found out she was pregnant, he blamed her for not being responsible and using contraception. He should have known when she'd lost her virginity to him that she wasn't worldly about that sort of thing. And her parents sure hadn't prepared her for that kind of situation.

However, instead of standing up for herself to her parents and Monroe, she pulled inward and just tried to shield herself and her baby from their verbal and emotional blows. Those blows rained down on her until she finally moved out on her own and got a job after leaving college mid-semester.

After drying her eyes, she lifted her head and looked around. Maybe some food would help. Thinking about it, she actually couldn't remember when she last ate. Oh yeah, it was at *It's A Grind*. It seemed like hours ago!

She looked over at the clock on the wall. It **had** been hours ago! Well, no wonder she was hungry!

She headed into the kitchen and started the coffee maker. The aroma of the freshly brewed coffee seemed to help her headache. She made herself a comfort sandwich; PB&J. With extra PB and more than the usual amount of J. it was perfect and just what she needed.

After cleaning up from her snack, Wren decided to take a break from her worries and read a book.

But the thought of reading a book brought her around full circle to the problem at the library!

Aaargh!

Dom asked the captain if he could run an idea by him.

The captain had been looking for a good excuse to get off his feet for a couple of minutes, and Dom's request happened at the perfect time for him.

They were in the office with the door closed while Dom explained what he wanted to do.

He knew the captain would grant his request if he could since the man felt just as guilty as he did about having to close the library.

"A calendar fundraiser? How would that work?"

Dom went on to explain it had originally been Mrs. Abbott's idea. At the statement, the captain's eyebrows shot up to the top of his forehead.

"That sweet old lady thought of this? A calendar of our firefighters? I mean I've heard of those calendars being very successful, but isn't that taking things a little too far?

Dom plowed ahead. "Not at all. Let me explain in full before you make any decisions."

"Okay, go for it."

Dom spent the next ten minutes selling the captain on the idea for the fundraiser. They could take preorders at a slight discount so people would give them the money up front. That money would then be used right away to pay for the repairs and upgrades at the library immediately. When the calendar was finished, the price would go up, and they would make money from that also.

He continued. Dom had already spoken with the local printing shop and they were willing to format everything and print the calendars at cost. They were also willing to wait for their payment until after the calendars had gone live, which would be helpful to the cause.

He finished up by explaining that the photographer was willing to take the pictures in exchange for the back page of the calendar cover to be used as a full page ad for the photographer's business. He'd even put a coupon on the advertisement so the calendars might sell even more.

At the end, the captain couldn't see a downside to it at all. In fact, Mrs. Abbott had come up with a brilliant plan.

But just how were they going to presell enough calendars to cover the cost of the repairs?

Dom hadn't figured out that part completely yet.

He had to speak with Shea's boyfriend about it first.

But he thought it might actually succeed!

Now to put out the word on the street that a firefighters' calendar was in the works!

Chapter Fourteen

"He's doing what?!" Wren just couldn't believe what Mrs. Abbott was telling her.

"I said, Dom is doing a calendar as a fundraiser to help the library." She took a sip from the cup sitting in front of her.

"A firefighter calendar?" Wren was fuming. She'd seen those beefcake calendars before and was appalled they were going to have pictures of them, bare chested even, for everyone to see.

Oh sure, she enjoyed looking at them herself, however they were NOT the right thing to use for fundraising for a public library!

Besides, Dom would be on one of the pages, wearing just a smile. Down deep inside she really didn't want other women to see him that way. Wren knew she'd pushed him away, but at the same time, she didn't want anyone else to have him in their life.

"What's the matter, Dear?" Mrs. Abbott pretended concern by showing a small gathering of wrinkles between her eyebrows.

Wren's jaw slowly dropped open from its clenched position. How could Mrs. Abbott possibly think this was a good idea!

"I'm really struggling with the fact that you seem to think a calendar of naked men is the appropriate vehicle to raise funds for the library!"

The woman set her cup down before leaning forward and taking Wren's hand in her own.

"Dear? Are you aware of just how priggish you sound?"

It took Wren a moment to understand what Mrs. Abbott had just said because she'd said it in such a loving and caring way, she hadn't been ready for the chastisement.

When it hit her, all she could do was sit there silently as she finally processed it.

Then a smile crossed her face.

Then she chuckled.

Then Wren opened her mouth and laughed so hard she couldn't catch her breath.

Mrs. Abbott just smiled, picked up her coffee and took another sip while Wren went through minutes of laughing, chuckling, holding her sides because they hurt, and apparently some inner contemplation between more bouts of laughing.

When the laughter finally subsided, Mrs. Abbott responded, "Actually, they're not naked."

The two women's eyes met and they both shared a chuckle.

After a moment, Wren asked, "But do you believe this is a fundraiser that would help us?"

"I certainly do. If the fire department takes preorders, and broadly publicizes what the money will be used for, we could have the funds we need within just a few days! I certainly think this is best and fastest route for us to take."

Wren sat back in the chair where, unbeknownst to her, Dom had sat just hours before. "If you think it would be all right, then I guess it's okay."

"Good! Then I'll contact the fire department and let them know they have the green light.

Wren got back home just in time to greet Caleb from his outing with Wylie and the boy's family. He was happy and exhausted, which suited her just fine. Maybe he would go to bed early tonight!

She turned to Wylie's mom to thank the couple for including Caleb for the day when the woman spoke up excitedly instead.

"Did you hear about the firefighter calendar fundraiser for the library?"

Just how fast IS the local gossip line anyway?

Wylie's dad just rolled his eyes at his wife's apparent enthusiasm.

"How did you find out?" Wren wasn't certain that she was comfortable with the speed this was all happening. Oh sure, she wanted to get the repairs done as soon as possible, but the method of funding it was still sticking with her.

"Oh, Wren, it's all over the place! I got text messages from another friend who is a clerk for the city council." She was almost jumping up and down in excitement. "I think this is a great idea! You must be so happy for the help!"

"Yes." That was all she was able to answer. "Yes, the funding will help immensely."

Even to herself, Wren sounded like a prim librarian.

After finally saying goodbye to everyone, Wren sent Caleb to go brush his teeth and get ready for bed.

After tucking him in, she went to bed herself.

She finally closed her eyes, only to be caught up in dreams of Dom posing for pictures.

It was not a restful sleep.

Wren woke up groggily to her cell phone ringing on her nightstand.

She glanced at the time when she picked the phone up to answer it.

8:30! She'd overslept, which instantly put her into an even worse mood than she'd been in last night.

"What!" Her one word question came across as an inquisition with her voice still gravelly and low from sleep.

There was a pause at the other end of the line.

"Ms. Johnson?"

"Yes. Who's calling?"

The man explained. "My name is Craig. I'm a reporter with a local news station. I would like to ask you some questions."

If he were able to see the frown that transformed Wren's face, he would have backed away, apologizing for disturbing her. But he couldn't, so he plowed on when she didn't answer. "It's about the Largo Bay Fire Department's fundraiser for the repairs that are needed at the library. I was told that the firefighter who came up with the idea was a friend of yours and I wanted to get your opinion on the project. You know. To add some color to the story."

Again, she didn't answer.

"Ms. Johnson? Are you still there?"

She thought about just hanging up on the man, but figured he'd just keep calling back.

"I'm sorry. What did you say your name was?"

"It's Craig, ma'am."

Whether he knew it or not, he'd just ensured there was no way he was going to get a comment of any sort out of Wren.

Ma'am! No one called a thirty-something woman *Ma'am* without repercussions of some sort.

"I'm sorry, but I can't." Wren was not about to get into detail about why she couldn't say anything. Especially with a complete stranger. "Please don't call back."

And with that, she disconnected the call.

Then she went back into her phone and blocked his phone number.

Feeling a little better, she got up and put on her robe and slippers.

She headed down the hallway to Caleb's room to see if he was awake yet.

He wasn't in bed, so she continued on into the living room and then into the kitchen.

There he was. He was already up and dressed! And it even looked like he'd already had a bowl of cereal for breakfast.

"Hey there, Mom!" He broke into a grin when he spotted her standing in the doorway. "If you show me how to make your coffee I can start doing that in the mornings for you!"

When did her little boy grow up so fast? Wren smiled and walked over to give him a hug.

"Have I ever told you that you are the world's best son?"

"Yeah. Plenty of times." He hugged her back. "But you can say it whenever you want."

"Since it's Sunday, would you like to go to the park?"

"Could Wylie come over here, instead?"

"Sure. If it's okay with his parents."

Maybe it was going to turn out to be a good day after all.

Chapter Fifteen

Caleb and Wylie had just finished putting together a space city when there was a knock on the door.

Wren got up from the couch where she'd been reading her favorite author and crossed to the door. Looking through the peephole, she saw a man she'd never seen before.

"Who is it?" she called through the door.

"Ms. Johnson?"

Wren immediately recognized the voice as belonging to the man who'd called and woken her up that morning, Craig.

"What do you want?" She still didn't open the door.

"Could I please have a minute of your time?"

"Why?" She knew why but wanted him to have to say it anyway. If she'd only known the man had skin as thick as an Army tank, she wouldn't have bothered even talking to him.

"It will just take a moment, Ms. Johnson." He sounded sincere, which unfortunately Wren gave him the benefit of the doubt and unlocked the door and opened it.

Immediately there was some commotion while the cameraman moved into position to film their conversation.

It startled Wren and she froze in place while they started filming.

And Craig's whole demeanor changed in an instant as he thrust a microphone into her face.

"So tell me, Ms. Johnson, is it true that the firefighter who is running this fundraiser for you is your boyfriend? Will he be making any money from it? How much does he plan to raise? Will the library actually see any of the funds?"

Wren stood frozen to the spot with his insinuated accusations and tone of voice.

"Mom? Who is it?" Unknown to Wren, Caleb had joined her at the open door when he heard a strange voice almost yelling at his mom.

Seeing the cameraman change his angle and start filming Caleb was all it took to wrench her out of her stupor.

She slammed the door and locked it.

When the men outside started knocking on the door again, she swiftly moved over and closed the drapes in case they were going to try to peer through her windows.

She waved for Caleb and Wylie, who were both grinning at the excitement, to follow her down the hallway as she headed to close all the other drapes.

"Mom!" Caleb had caught up with her. "What did that man want?"

"He's a reporter." She left that room and headed to her bedroom almost at a run.

Both boys were having a good time with all the action taking place and stayed on Wren's heels as she sped around the apartment.

"Is the firefighter he's talking about, Dom?" Caleb had heard every word. And being as bright as he was, it didn't take much to put everything he'd overheard last night with Wylie's mom and now this morning.

Wren really did not want to answer that question, but knew she needed to be honest with her son.

"Yes. The reporter was trying to say that Dom was going to take some of the money from the fire department's fundraiser for the library repairs."

"He'd never do that!" Caleb raised himself to his full height in outrage. "Dom is a good guy."

"Yes. Of course he is." Wren pulled the blinds down in the kitchen and sat down at the table. The boys both joined her.

"Just because an adult says something is true, doesn't mean it's really true." Wren then added to her statement, "Good people don't make up bad things about other people and spread it around."

The boys nodded solemnly as though taking in words of wisdom, which they actually were.

"Do you understand?" Wren didn't want to burden them with worry, but she also didn't want to pretend everything was okay.

"Yes." Caleb and Wylie both nodded in unison. Wren smiled at how cute they both looked.

She smiled right up until Caleb asked, "Is Dom your boyfriend like the man said?"

She wasn't sure how she could answer that without emotion flooding her already stressed psyche. So instead, she asked, "You guys want some hot dogs for lunch?"

And of course, they did.

Dom was the last one to arrive at Max's that afternoon for his sister's birthday party. He leaned into the backseat and grabbed the balloon bouquet he'd brought for the occasion. He'd wanted to get there earlier but had to finish some paperwork at the station first.

He walked into the house and was first greeted by the birthday girl herself.

Shea laughed when she saw the enormous number of balloons he'd purchased.

"You didn't have to do this!" Shea took the ribbons holding the balloons from Dom's outstretched hand. "But I'm glad you did!" She gave him a kiss on the cheek. "They're gorgeous."

"And much better than some awful coffee mug with a saying on it that points out the fact that you're getting older." Max came through the door from the kitchen and laughed when he saw the balloons were taking up at least five square feet of his living room.

"From all the cars outside, it looks like there must by at least thirty people here!" Dom had noticed that almost every curb along the street had a car parked next to it.

"Oh. No. Most of them are at a bar-be-que down the street. That new couple moved in a month ago, and this must be their welcome home party." Max had received an invitation to it, but after they'd already scheduled Shea's party, he'd sent his regrets instead.

He added, "Come on into the dining room! We're ready to eat."

Max headed back to the dining table and Shea and Dom followed him.

Dom made the rounds and gave and got handshakes and hugs from everyone. Meeting Zach, he instantly felt a connection even though the guy was in the music business, not public service.

He finally sat in his chair and Max had them all join hands to say grace before they started the meal.

Chapter Sixteen

Max sat back from his plate and gave a huge sigh of satisfaction.

"Erin, you outdid yourself once again."

Murmurs of agreement from the others at the table immediately followed his announcement.

"Thank you! I think that means I get to sit here while someone else clears the table and cleans up in the kitchen, eh?" Erin grinned across the table at Charlie and Bobby who hadn't been able to take their eyes off each other the entire meal.

Dom, who'd been sitting next to them cleared his throat in a pointed manner to get their attention.

"Oh! Yes, of course we'll do the dishes." Charlie couldn't hide her blush when she realized she and Bobby had gotten caught … again. She stood up and Bobby joined her immediately in grabbing empty plates from the table.

Shea leaned forward and looked across Luca at Zach. "So, what's the news about Luca's recording?" Everyone else at the table quit speaking among themselves and listened also.

Zach's face showed that he was interested in what they would all think at his announcement. He hadn't even told Luca yet!

"Dude! I know you weren't expecting this but I know that you'll be totally stoked!" He watched Luca's grin spread even wider, as though he knew what was coming. "I know you think you know what this is, but it's even better than that."

"Well don't keep us waiting!" Shea demanded as she reached across and gave Zach's shoulder a small punch.

Zach laughed while he rubbed his shoulder as though it had actually hurt. "Ow! Luca, tell your girlfriend to stop hitting me."

"Well then I suggest you better tell us!"

As everyone around the table settled down Zach leaned forward and made the announcement, "There is a million dollar contract just waiting for Luca to sign."

The table was silent. Even Max's mouth had dropped open.

Finally, Luca asked in a whisper, "Did you say one million dollars?"

Zach's grin couldn't get any wider. "Yep. And ... wait for it ... that's just the signing bonus."

Shea glanced between Luca and Zach trying to take in what was being said. Did that mean the contract was going to be for more money than one million dollars?

Zach started to chuckle. Then Luca joined him. Paul seemed to be one of the first of the others to catch on and he was smiling too and nodding.

Shea touched Luca's hand and he turned to her asking, "Baby, do you know what this means?" Then he kissed her quickly on the mouth before adding, "We're rich!"

He could tell from her uncertain expression that it hadn't completely sunk in yet. He took both her hands in his and whispered, "Shea, I made it."

Her face cleared and she seemed to understand as her eyes started to shine.

Luca jumped to his feet and pulled her up with him in an embrace. "We did it." Then he turned to Zach, "WE did it!"

Zach just sat back enjoying the expanding reaction his words had created. It was such a joy to watch as everyone finally, to some extent, started to realize what had just happened.

Max was up and out of his chair. "Congratulations, Luca!" He reached out and shook the man's hand. Then he hugged his daughter, Shea. "I'm so happy for you!"

"Happy for me? Why?" Shea actually sounded puzzled.

Max looked at Luca for a moment then stepped back as the young man reached out again and took Shea's hand in his and gazed directly into her eyes.

Nudges, smiles, and nods circled the table before he dropped to one knee in front of her.

Shea was still bewildered at what was taking place. Why was Luca on his knee? Why was he gazing at her with his eyes filled with adoration and ... *Oh!*

It was almost too much for her to take in. Her breath caught in her throat and tears started to burn her eyes. Did she really want this? The answer that immediately came to mind was *Yes! Definitely, yes.*

Luca saw the acceptance of his as-yet-unstated proposal and took a deep breath before speaking.

"Miss Shea Bella McGannon. Mi Bella. Would you do me the honor of becoming my wife? I love you. I will take care of you throughout our lives. I want to have children with you. I want to grow old together with you. Will you marry me?"

There was not a dry eye in the house.

Although it seemed like an eternity before Shea answered, it was actually only a few seconds.

"Yes, Luca. I would love to marry you."

He started to get up off his knee in order to seal their agreement with a kiss, but she stopped him by adding more.

"I will also take care of you. I can't wait to have children with you and I'm looking forward to growing old together. I think we will create a wonderful family."

He stood up the rest of the way and took her into his arms before slowly kissing her. Everyone else stood up and applauded and cheered.

The kiss ended and Shea looked around the table at her family. When she got to her dad, she realized something.

"I can't leave the department! You need me there."

"Yes, that's true, I do need you there."

Luca looked at his future father-in-law with concern before Max added, "But I'd rather have some grandchildren!" He glanced around the table at his other kids. "You guys are taking too long for my contentment!"

Everyone laughed at his pointed remark.

Zach added, "Shea? Have you ever considered private security work? Luca's going to need a bodyguard or two."

When her eyes clouded with worry, Zach hurried to reassure her. "It's just for show. There won't be any problems."

She looked at Luca. "Promise?"

"I promise." He was not going to give her any more cause for unease. He shot a look of *what-the-heck?!* at Zach who nodded back in understanding.

Dom broke the somber mood by asking, "Does this mean you might be able to help with the financing for the library's repairs?"

Everyone laughed, thinking Dom was joking.

No. He was serious. He needed to get some money fast in order to help Wren. She wouldn't even speak with him right now, and he knew the only way she'd let him back into her and Caleb's lives was to help with getting the library back open. In fact, he thought it was his only chance.

"Well, I don't have the money yet, but what if we scheduled a local performance with all the proceeds going toward the library? Do you think that might work?" Luca wanted to help.

His offer got everyone talking again, trying to figure out how to get it up and running in the least amount of time.

The first thing was setting the date for the concert. They all agreed if they worked together they'd be able to get the venue, permits, and flyers posted all over town before the next weekend.

By the end of the evening, they all had their marching orders and agreed to check in with each other the next evening.

Luca and Shea were standing at her front door, saying goodnight.

"I don't want to say goodbye yet."

"I don't either."

Shea looked up into his eyes and asked, "How are we going to make this work?"

"What do you mean?" Luca wrapped his arms around her and rested his chin on the top of her head.

"You'll be on tour most of the time and I'll be on duty." She sighed and snuggled into his embrace.

He leaned back a little; just enough to look into her eyes. "We'll work it out. No matter what comes up, we'll work together and figure it out. Now, tell me you believe me."

His smile and promise was all she needed. "I believe you."

Shea gave Luca another kiss before adding, "Would you like to come in?"

Luca struggled to understand what she was offering when she added, "For a cup of coffee?"

He relaxed and dragged his arms from around her. As much as his body was shouting *yes*, he knew he wanted to do the right thing by her, and her family as well.

"I think I need to get home. It's getting late."

"Okay." She gave him an impish smile. "Sweet dreams."

"Oh, you have no idea!" Luca laughed and took a step back. "See you tomorrow?"

"Tomorrow." Shea watched him turn and walk down the sidewalk to his vehicle. He got there and waved again. She waved back but didn't go inside until he'd gotten the car started and put it into gear. She knew Luca would sit there until he knew she was safe.

And that made her feel cherished.

Chapter Seventeen

Wren was dumbfounded when she saw the flyer taped to the light pole downtown. A charity concert? For her library? This coming weekend? Wow!

How did someone get Luca Napier, the recording artist, to perform in Largo Bay? What was his connection to the library? And why was he doing it?

She knew she needed some answers, but at the moment was thrilled it was taking place.

She was on her way to pick up Caleb from school, and just happened to take a route through the downtown area.

By accident.

Not on purpose.

It wasn't like she was going to drive past the fire department because she knew it was there!

No. It just occurred to be a coincidence that her route today led her past Dom's place of work.

It had slipped her mind he even worked there! In fact, she'd forgotten all about him.

Wren sighed in frustration. She'd been trying so hard this past week to really, truly learn to hate the man. But then she'd remember something he'd done to help Caleb and all her barriers against him crumbled.

Just what was it that made her feel like she was a moth being drawn to his flame? Okay, that was a little over the top.

Just what was it that made it impossible to forget him?

Yes. That was better.

She rolled her eyes as she stated out loud, "I need to stop having these conversations with myself." When she heard the words echo inside the car, she cringed.

Geez, I'm going to end up as an old lady with five dozen cats inhabiting my house if I keep this up.

But it was all Dom's fault!

If he hadn't shown up that day at her apartment, looking for some letters she'd found at the thrift store, none of her problems would be happening.

Liar.

Wren huffed and set her mouth in a straight line. She really disliked it when her inner voice was right.

Then there he was. Standing in the fire department's wide driveway as she drove past. He was washing one of the fire engines with a long-handled brush.

And he looked just like what he was, a hero. All he needed was a white stallion and a suit of armor. Or maybe a cowboy hat. Or perhaps a white lab coat with a stethoscope around his neck. Wren sighed as her imagination took flight.

This was going to be a very long day.

"Hey! Wasn't that Wren?" One of his buddies got Dom's attention with his shout.

"Where?" Dom turned around to see what his friend was talking about, but only caught the back of her car heading down the road.

He stood there, watching her drive away. Man, he sure hoped the money for the library's repairs would put him back in good standing with her and Caleb.

It just had to.

Wren drove up to the school, but Caleb wasn't waiting for her by the front steps like he usually did. The only person standing outside was the director of the academy. She motioned for Wren to park her car and come inside.

When Wren reached the director, she noticed the look of concern on the woman's face and felt her stomach clench up.

"Is Caleb all right?" Wren was breathless with worry.

"Oh, yes he is." They walked toward the office area. "I kept him inside with my assistant."

"Is he in trouble?"

"Caleb? Never!" The woman smiled.

"Oh. " Wren was puzzled. "Why is he being kept inside?"

Just then they rounded the hallway corner and entered the office.

"Mom!" Caleb jumped up from the chair he was in. "You'll never guess who's here!" This was the absolute happiest she'd ever seen her son.

She looked up from him as a man rose from the chair next to where Caleb had been sitting. At first she didn't recognize him, it had been so long since she'd last seen him.

But then it hit her.

The man was Caleb's biological father.

The ringing in Wren's ears got louder and wouldn't stop as she felt dizzy and her eyes closed.

From far away, she heard the school's director say "Oh, no!"

She felt herself drifting downward, as though floating on a cloud.

When she finally came to, she was on a cot in a room at the school nurse's office. There was a light blanket covering her. Through the open doorway she could barely hear voices.

It sounded like the director was speaking to a man.

But, when she heard Caleb say the word "Dad" she sat up immediately as everything came flooding back to her.

"Caleb?" She called out to her son. When he didn't hear her, she cleared her throat and called again.

He popped up in the doorway. "Mom! You're awake! Dad told me you just needed a little nap before we left."

By this time, she'd sat up and straightened her clothes and hair.

Caleb hopped up next to her on the cot and threw his arms around her.

"I'm okay, Caleb. Just needed a little rest."

"Oh, I already knew that. I was hugging you because Dad showed up! He said it had taken him a very long time to find us, which was why he hadn't been with us earlier."

"Really?" Wren was trying to hold back her anger at the man just showing up out of the blue without even warning her ahead of time. "What else did he say?"

"That I was so sorry I couldn't find you sooner." Stan Auerbach stood in the doorway looking like a model on the cover of GQ magazine. He was even posed, casually of course, in a very attractive stance. And he knew it. He'd practiced in front of a full-length mirror long enough.

The director appeared in the doorway next to him.

"Would you like me to take Caleb to the cafeteria for a snack?" Her eyes showed her concern.

"Yes please." Wren answered before Stan could say another word. "Caleb, please go with her. I'll be right here when you get back."

Caleb hopped off the cot and followed the woman out.

Wren looked down at her clenched hands before looking up at him and asked, "Why are you here?"

Stan gave her a look of feigned surprise. "Why wouldn't I be here? The boy is my son."

"The *boy's* name is Caleb. And you are not named on the birth certificate."

"I know. That's just an oversight that can be fixed easily enough." He sounded almost bored with the conversation, which made Wren's anger bubble to the surface.

"I repeat, why are you here?"

"Oh, Wren. Don't be like that." She'd seen this pleading little boy look from him before. In fact, it was right before she'd given herself to him, thinking they were going to get married. This time, it didn't sway her one bit. In fact, it gave her strength when she realized just how much she'd grown since last being with him.

"You can skip the acting, Stan. I've developed immunity to it over the past years. Just tell me why you're here." Before he could open his mouth, she added, "And don't lie this time."

The look on his face instantly changed to a dark scowl.

"Wow. It looks like someone has grown a backbone ... or maybe it's a set of claws."

If he'd hoped to make her back down, he'd failed miserably. In fact, he'd given her even more energy to fight him.

Wren stood up, a bored look on her face.

"Oh, please. Let's just get this over with so you can leave."

He stood up straighter.

"I'm not leaving, Wren."

She gave him a wary side glance as he continued.

"At least, not without the boy."

Chapter Eighteen

Wren had finally gotten Caleb to settle down and go to sleep for the night. It had taken almost two hours!

And now she sat at her kitchen table, wondering what she was going to do.

Should she just pack up and disappear? It only took her a moment to scratch that idea. If Stan had tracked them down once, he could do it again. Especially with all his family's money and connections.

Wren knew she couldn't afford to fight him in court. She didn't have the resources. When he'd threatened to do just that if she didn't hand over Caleb by the end of the week, she knew there was no way she could let that happen.

She just didn't know what she could do about it.

Wasn't there a group in town where she could get some legal advice for just a small fee, or even better, no cost at all?

When she finally glanced at the clock, she was surprised to find it was after one in the morning!

She had to get to bed. The problem was, she wasn't tired. Angry? Of course. Lost? You bet. Feeling helpless? Almost.

She came to a decision. First thing in the morning, she'd call Mrs. Abbott and see if she and Caleb could visit for the day. Wren knew she'd want to help as soon as she heard what was about to occur with Caleb.

Just that small decision helped Wren fall asleep; after she'd double checked that all the windows and the front door were locked and secure for the night.

Mrs. Abbott had just set up Caleb in her outside back screened room with the modeling clay Wren had brought with them that morning.

She'd also left a plate of cookies and a glass of water with the boy.

She rejoined Wren in the parlor and sat next to her on the couch.

"Okay, my dear. Spill it. I want to hear everything that is on your mind." She sat back on the couch with her mug of coffee and waited for Wren to start.

She'd expected the young woman to confess her hidden love for Dom any moment. When Wren started in with "Caleb's father found us" she couldn't hide her surprise.

"Oh my! Forgive me, but I thought he was dead." At least that was what she'd been led to believe by others in town.

Wren shrugged in resignation.

"That's what I wanted everyone to believe; that I was a widow." Then she added in a smaller voice, "It just seemed easier that way."

"Please, Wren. Start at the beginning. If I understand everything, maybe I'll be able to help. And believe me, I will not be judging anything you have to say. Earlier in my life, some things occurred that I wished hadn't. But I've learned to live with my regrets. Please don't live the rest of yours the way I have."

Wren just looked at the older woman in surprise. She'd assumed Mrs. Abbott was a widow with grown children living somewhere else. It had never occurred to her that there was more to it than that.

"I know. I appear to be a mild-mannered, contented old woman. Please listen to me. Everyone has a past. Not one single person has lived a perfect life. If they say they have, they are lying, either to you or to themselves. And here's another shocker! Every old person was once young, also. We all were children. We all went through our adolescent years with angst, tears, and sometimes triumphs. We all fell in love. Sometimes, we were lucky enough to find the right person. Sometimes we weren't and lived to our dying day regretting our choices."

Wren reached across the couch and took her hand.

Mrs. Abbott looked up at Wren and continued, "Please give me the chance to help you and your wonderful Caleb. I will do whatever I can to see you happy with your life. It would give me a second chance to maybe become part of a family if you will allow me to be part of yours."

They both had tears in their eyes by the time she'd finished.

Wren swallowed hard before answering, "Of course." Then she sat up straighter. "In fact, you'll be the first person I've ever told the whole story to."

Mrs. Abbott laughed and answered, "Excellent! In that case, let's get started." And she grabbed another cookie for herself as she got ready to listen.

Wren started at the beginning, when she entered middle school when she first realized that she had not been living up to her parents' expectations. No, in fact she'd been failing miserably.

It took the better part of an hour, and a fresh pot of coffee, as well as another plate of cookies, for her story to finally arrive at present day. During the entire recitation, Mrs. Abbott responded with despair, anger, tears, and even cheered once when Wren told her what she'd said to Stanley at the school.

"Good for you! You stood up to him! That showed gumption." Then she added, "I'm very proud of you."

The women hugged before wiping their eyes and taken sips from their coffee.

Mrs. Abbott was determined to help. This time she wasn't going to be shamed into walking away from a situation. No, this time, she'd do what she knew was right.

"Hey, Mom!" Caleb came into the room. "Wanta come see what I made?" He looked excited to show her, so she stood up and followed him to the back porch.

While Wren and Caleb were in the back, Mrs. Abbott got out her phone and made a call.

"Domingo, we have to talk. Can you come by for dinner tonight?" She listened to his answer and smiled. "Excellent! See you then."

She'd put away her phone before Wren called down the hallway. "Mrs. Abbott, please come see what Caleb created!"

She smiled to herself and got up from the couch slowly. Some days her hips didn't work as well as other days, but that wasn't about to slow her down. Not for one minute.

Not when this young woman and her child needed her help.

Chapter Nineteen

Dom ended the call with Mrs. Abbott, assuring her he'd be there around seven. He hadn't heard her sound that energetic ever before. He sure hoped she'd thought of a way to help him get back into Wren's life.

He knew he'd made a huge mistake not telling her immediately about the needed repairs to the library. It was just that he was enjoying being around her and Caleb so much, he didn't want to ruin everything.

Well, not being open and honest with her had created the very thing he was trying to avoid. So, he'd made himself a promise that no matter what might happen, from here on out he'd tell her everything. He needed her to trust him again or they wouldn't have any chance whatsoever to move forward.

Watching Luca ask Shea to marry him had given Dom an entirely new viewpoint on where he wanted his life to go.

He'd finally admitted to himself that he wanted what his parents had; a loving relationship built on trust and love, as well as a house full of children. Dom knew he'd adopt Caleb just as soon as he asked Wren to marry him.

But first, he had to get her to be willing to at least talk to him, much less accept him as her fiancé.

He figured after his shift ended, he'd have just time to go home, shower, and still make it to Mrs. Abbott's place on time.

He sure hoped she had more of those cookies for dessert.

Wren was just setting dinner on the table for her and Caleb when there was a knock at her door. She asked Caleb if he'd get their ice waters for their dinner and headed over to the door.

She looked through the peephole but didn't recognize the man. He had on a uniform of some sort and was writing on a clipboard.

She thought he looked safe, so she opened the door, but left the new chain attached.

"Yes? May I help you?" Wren asked.

"Are you…" The man glanced again at the front of a large envelope before continuing, "Ms. Wren Johnson?"

"Yes, I am."

"Good. This is for you." He handed the envelope through the wedge of open door, then announced, "You've been served." He grinned at her, turned around and went back to what was apparently his car, sitting at the curb.

Served? With what? After closing and locking the door behind her, Wren took the envelope back into the kitchen with her.

She swore she was not going to be so naïve in the future about people. That man hadn't been safe at all.

"What is it, Mom?" Caleb had already started eating the meatloaf on his plate after covering it with at least an inch of ketchup.

"I'm not sure." She didn't open it, but instead set it on the windowsill to open after they'd finished their meal.

Smiling at the amount of condiment Caleb was using, Wren picked up her own fork and took a bite of the new meatloaf recipe she'd tried.

Caleb watched while she silently chewed and swallowed.

Then he laughed when she picked up the ketchup bottle and slathered her plate with it also.

It was better with the red stuff on it. In fact, you could hardly even taste what was under it.

Dom added a little salt to the mashed potatoes Mrs. Abbott had put on his plate. She pretended not to notice, since she actually agreed with his assessment after taking a bite, herself.

"Oh, shoot! I forgot to add the butter and salt to the potatoes!" She got up and went into the kitchen, bringing back the butter dish. "Help yourself!"

Dom laughed. "I'm glad it wasn't just my palate that thought something was maybe lacking."

She gave him a wry smile and added both butter and salt to her own mound of white stuff before putting a forkful into her own mouth.

Dom took a drink of water to wash down the remainder from his last bite before asking her a question.

"So. Any news?"

Mrs. Abbott shoved another bite into her mouth before answering. It took her several seconds to finish eating it and then taking a drink of water from her glass.

Dom was starting to think she'd done it on purpose to keep from answering.

Actually, she was just pulling her thoughts together on how to proceed.

Finally, she answered. "Dom? Don't you have a sister who is an attorney?"

That wasn't even close to what he thought she'd invited him to dinner to discuss.

"I do! Her name is Char." He paused with the fork halfway to his mouth, then set it down. "Do you need an attorney?"

"No. But someone you care very much for does."

It took Dom a while to drag everything out of her, but he finally did. And he was enraged! An ex-boyfriend? Caleb's father? Why now? What did the jerk want? These questions swirled through his mind as Mrs. Abbott retrieved their ice cream and cookies from the kitchen.

She placed his bowl in front of him and pushed the plate of cookies close to the bowl.

Dom stared down at the dessert that had just been presented to him. Then he looked back up at Mrs. Abbott.

"Why aren't you as upset as I am?"

"Oh, believe me, Dom. I am." She picked up a cookie and started to nibble on it. "I've just had more time to process everything. Give it a little while to settle. Have some ice cream."

And that is just what he did. The fact he was chewing it with ferocity wasn't missed by the woman sitting across from him.

Oh, how she hoped she hadn't made a mistake getting him involved with Wren's legal problems. She would surely regret it if she had.

Chapter Twenty

Wren finally got a chance to open the envelope after getting Caleb to bed that evening. Truthfully, all she wanted to do was to go to bed herself. What would it hurt to leave the envelope intact until morning, anyway?

But she knew herself well enough to know she wouldn't sleep at all, tossing and turning with worry and curiosity.

So, she made herself a cup of chamomile tea and settled into the corner of the couch, as though she could sort of hide from whatever words were on the pages enclosed.

She slit open the envelope and pulled out the papers.

It was a pretty hefty stack. She could immediately tell they were legal papers from the paper it was printed on.

What was that called? Oh yeah. Pleading paper.

Wren could only shake her head at the absurd things she was able to remember from her days at college, but not the things she needed to be able to recall for day-to-day life. Like her dentist's last name.

She realized she was procrastinating and started to read the first page of the first document.

After twenty minutes of legal reading, she came to the conclusion that she was being sued for several things.

But the weird thing was that she wasn't being sued by Stanley, but by his parents!

Wren could barely recall them, except for the way they made her feel as though she was inferior to them when Stanley had invited her to dinner at their house right after they'd met.

She picked up the fourth document to start reading it, but realized she was too tired to continue.

The one thing she knew with certainty was she needed a lawyer if she was going to be able to win against them.

Not only did they want the right to see their grandson on a regular basis, but they also wanted reimbursement for damages for each year they claimed she'd kept Caleb from them.

They hadn't wanted her! Especially after they found out she was pregnant with their son's child.

No, it was just the opposite. They refused to have her in their lives. They'd made that abundantly clear at the time.

But Wren also knew they had connections at some prominent levels and was afraid she'd be sucked into the legal tangle of the good-old-boys-club. And maybe lose Caleb.

No, that couldn't be allowed to happen.

She went to bed, praying she'd be able to get at least four hours of sleep before having to make it through the next day with everything that was going on.

Wren had gotten Caleb to school on time the next day and had even been able to let the director know that the man she met the day before yesterday had no legal claim to Caleb and should not be allowed to see him or take him from the school.

She filled out the form the school secretary handed her and headed back to her car feeling better about Caleb being at school.

At least she didn't have to worry about Stanley trying to take him physically.

She arrived home and sat down in one of the kitchen chairs, once again looking over the legal documents that had been served on her yesterday.

It irked her that the service agent had seemed to enjoy the whole thing a little too much. How could anyone enjoy a job like that? Didn't the man have even an ounce of empathy for the people being served with perhaps a life-altering document?

Come on, Wren! Get it together. Think! What is your next step?

She started to get up to go to her computer to research legal help when her phone rang.

She didn't recognize the number on her screen, but it was a local one, so she picked up.

"Hello?"

A woman's voice replied, "Is this Wren?"

"Um, yes?" Wren had no idea who she was.

"Wren, my name is Char McGannon. I'm an attorney."

McGannon? Like in Dom McGannon?

"Um, okay." Wren was even more hesitant to speak with the woman now.

"I understand that you're uncertain if you should speak with me. You don't know me at all. However, I received a call this morning indicating that you might need some legal help."

Wren started to tell the woman to leave her alone, but thankfully was able to realize that yes, she **did** need legal help.

Instead, she asked, "Are you related to Dom McGannon?"

This time, Char hesitated. She knew Wren was really upset with Dom about something. At least that's what he'd told her last night. But she wasn't exactly sure how to answer if she was going to be able to help the woman. After all, her brother swore fealty to her if she'd only help in this one case. And it wasn't often a sibling, especially a younger one, pledged their lifetime loyalty.

"I am, Wren, but please don't hold that against me."

That made Wren smile. It seemed that another female also had difficulties with the man.

"Yes. Char was it?"

"Yes. You can also call me Charlie; the rest of the family does."

Wren was starting to like her already.

"Charlie, I do need help. I'm being sued and I don't know what to do."

"Can you meet me today around noon? I'll be at the *It's A Grind* for lunch if you're free."

"Yes, I can meet you. But..." Wren hesitated before continuing. "But I can't afford to pay a lot."

Now it was Char's turn to hedge a little bit. Dom had told her he'd pay for Wren's defense (at the family discount, of course.) But Char just knew the woman would turn her down if she knew about Dom paying. So instead, she fudged a little bit.

"That's okay. You actually don't have to pay anything at all. I am obliged to take a certain number of pro bono cases every year, so you're covered." If Wren only knew Char had already taken on more than her fair share over the past year, she might not believe her.

Then she heard the relief in Wren's voice, and it made everything all right in Char's world.

"Thank you. Thank you so much." Wren felt like the weight of the world had just been lifted a little bit.

"You're more than welcome. See you at noon."

Chapter Twenty-One

C har ended the call and turned to Dom who'd been sitting there the whole time.

"Is she going to take the offer?" Dom thought so but wanted to be sure.

"Yes, she is." Char smiled at the obvious easing of the worry he'd been dragging around behind him now for weeks.

"You seem pretty intense about her." Char was curious. "Anything more you might want me to know, little bro?"

Dom grinned at his sister. "You'll find out soon enough."

He stood up to leave, but first leaned down and gave her a quick hug.

"Thank you. I mean that."

Dom said it with all sincerity. Char could only believe that Wren was going to be part of the family pretty soon, so she better do a fantastic job with the legal case.

Char tried to keep her Scottish temper in check while looking over the documents. After all, they were out in public. But it hadn't taken much for her to see exactly what the man's family was trying to do to Wren. They were trying to overwhelm her so that she would sign away whatever parental rights they wanted her to.

"Do you understand what these say?" Char indicated the papers to Wren.

"I think so. At least most of it." Wren hoped Char would be able to clarify them into some sort of simpler form.

"There's something I don't understand about all of this." Char turned the papers face down on the table before she looked back up at Wren. "Why now?"

"What?" Wren didn't understand the question.

"Why are they suing you now, after all these years?"

Wren slowly shook her head while she searched for an answer. After coming up blank, she shrugged.

"Okay, but I'll bet we can figure out why now if we take a hard look at everything."

"Stanley said it was because they couldn't find me until now. That he'd been looking for me everywhere."

"Something about that just doesn't ring right. You have a driver's license, yes?"

"Of course."

"You have a social security number, right?"

"Right."

"Is your phone number unlisted?"

"No."

"So, that means Stanley is lying to you."

"But why would he lie?"

"I think the question should be 'why wouldn't he?'"

Wren shook her head in dismay. "Why do I always believe everything anyone else says?"

"Well, that can't be true." Char smiled. "I happen to know you don't believe what Dom tells you!"

Char's statement startled Wren out of her introspection. In fact, it was so true that Wren had to laugh.

"Yes. You are right. I don't give him the benefit of the doubt at all."

"Can't say I blame you."

Both women had a good laugh.

Also, they both felt like they might have found a new friend.

"So! What did she say?" Dom was fidgeting with anticipation.

"You know I can't say anything!" Char set down her briefcase on his couch. "Remember a little thing called attorney-client privilege?"

"You're kidding! I'm paying for your services!"

"That is certainly true. Please remind me to send an invoice for services rendered so far."

"Char?" His voice was almost a whine.

"No. Seriously. You're not my client, Dom. She is." Char patted her brother on the shoulder. "Hang in there. Without giving away any secrets, I can tell you that I know what to do with this case. By the way, I'm going to have to hire a private detective for some background research."

"On Wren?"

"No. On the man's family. There is something there that is not making sense."

"What's that?"

She patted him again. "Sorry. That's what I can't tell you. You got any coffee?"

Dom sulked. "You know how to make it. Help yourself."

Char just laughed all the way into the kitchen.

Yep, her brother had it pretty bad for the lady and her son.

Chapter Twenty-Two

Max and Zach were sitting at the kitchen table in Max's house.

Zach had just spent the second night there and he and Max had stayed up late, talking about politics, religion, sports, and every other subject that could have potentially caused an argument.

They were both surprised to find that they agreed on almost everything. Including the fact Shea and Luca actually made the perfect couple, despite their different careers.

Now, at this early morning hour, the men were discussing women. It had started off with Max telling Zach about his beloved Luz. By the time he was done extolling her virtues, Max realized he'd stopped referring to her in the present and was now speaking of her in the past.

It was an insight that had never crossed his mind before.

Hmmm. Maybe he was finally getting through the paralyzing grief he'd been trying to hide from everyone. He smiled to himself at his knew understanding of himself.

At first, after she'd died, he figured he would probably join her very soon. Then when that didn't happen, he assumed he'd live out the rest of his life as a shell of the man he'd once been. And then when that didn't happen, he didn't quite know what to do with himself.

He was thankful every single day for his children and their support. Looking back, he knew he could not have gotten through it without them.

He quietly hoped he'd been able to help them too in some way. Little did he know that his persistence in just showing up day after day is what had held the family together.

"So, Zach, any women in your life?" Max had just poured himself a fresh cup of coffee and was about to sit back down at the table when a thought struck him.

"Before you answer that question, let's move ourselves out to the porch where we can see the ocean."

Zach let out a silent sigh of relief at not having to respond right away. "That sounds great. Lead on."

The men grabbed their cups and ended up at the wraparound porch's back corner where all the cushioned chairs and couch were.

The view was spectacular. The sun had just come up over the horizon. There were some clouds partially covering it, so the beams weren't too bright. The light from it was just enough to catch the waves in the bay, making them look like diamonds floating in the sea.

After picking out and settling into a couple of comfy seats, Max repeated his question to Zach.

"What were we talking about? Oh, yeah. Women. Specifically, the women in **your** life."

Zach gave an uncomfortable chuckle before answering. "Actually, there's not much to tell."

Max's eyebrows shot up. "You're kidding! A young man like yourself with no women?"

Zach reacted fast to Max's comment. "Oh, no. There have been women." He rubbed the back of his neck before continuing. "Actually, there have been quite a few."

When he didn't go on, Max asked, "Anyone special?"

He watched as Zach's expression softened before he answered, "Yes. There was one."

"And?"

Zach looked up when he realized he'd mentally gone somewhere else. Somewhere in the past.

"She was someone special." Zach's soft tone told Max almost everything.

"And she's no longer around?"

"Unfortunately, no." He took a sip of his cooling coffee, not noticing the change, he was so lost in his thoughts.

"What was her name?" Max took a sip of his own coffee, grimaced at its lack of heat, and set the cup down.

A small smile made Zach look ten years younger for a moment.

"Her name is Rachel. We met about ten years ago at a concert." Zach could almost hear the band playing in his head.

"Were you together long?"

Now his smile faded.

"No. It was just that one night. After the concert we headed to the shoreline and spent the rest of the night talking and watching the moon over the ocean." He paused at the memory of it. "I'd never connected that strongly with anyone else in my life. Or since then, to be honest."

"Why didn't you see her again?" Now Max was intrigued.

Zach scowled. "Because I was young and dumb." He shook his head. "We agreed to meet for a bite to eat at a local breakfast diner. She wanted to go home and clean up first. I also thought that was a good idea, so we planned on meeting there in a couple of hours."

"I take it she didn't show up." Max figured he knew where this story was heading.

"NO! That's the worst part of the whole thing. **I** didn't show up. When I got home, I stretched out for just a moment, but fell asleep instead. When I finally made it to the diner, she wasn't there. The hostess confirmed Rachel had waited for over an hour." Zach grimaced. "She must have thought I was just stringing her along or something."

Max could feel the young man's pain emanating from him.

"Did you have her phone number?"

"No. And not even her last name. I didn't even know where she lived so I could track her down and apologize."

"Wow. That's not a happy story."

"It's haunted me ever since. She just seemed so perfect. It was as though we were old friends from way in the past." Zach laughed at himself. "I sound like some new-age hippie, don't I?"

"Not in the least." Max had that same connection with Luz, so he truly understood Zach's pain.

They sat there in silence for quite a while before heading back into the house to start their days.

The fire chief was grinning as he knocked on his office window, getting Dom's attention.

Dom trotted over and stuck his head in the door. "Morning!"

"Good morning, yourself! Come on in. Do I have some good news for you or what?" The chief could barely contain himself.

Dom walked in all the way and waited.

"We just got the first segment of preorders in for the calendar." He was holding a notepad in his hand and turned it around so Dom could see the figure.

Dom didn't think he'd read it right, so he reached out and brought the paper closer. Nope. He'd been right about the amount.

He looked up at the chief in awe. "How did that happen?"

The chief just shrugged. "Not sure. Maybe the marketing?"

"But this is twice the amount we needed for the library upgrades."

"Yep. Nice – eh?"

"Wow! This isn't just nice, it's fantastic!" Dom's grin matched his boss's.

"When can we get started?"

"I have to call the contractors for the various repairs and get them scheduled."

"Well, what are we waiting for? Can they start today?"

"Just hold your horses, Dom." He chuckled. "I just now got the notice. I'll make some calls today and get things started."

"Let me know if there is anything I can do to help speed things up!"

"I will. Now, get back to work. Those turnouts aren't going to inspect themselves."

Yes, the day was definitely looking much brighter!

What could possibly go wrong?

Chapter Twenty-Three

Stanley Auerbach's day was not going as he'd planned at all.

First, he'd gotten another call from his mother, which had gone to his voicemail because he did NOT want to speak with her. She was always nagging about how he hadn't done this or that thing correctly. About how he'd turned out to be a family failure and a disappointment.

For Stan, being that last item was the worst. If he disappointed his parents again, they'd told him in no uncertain terms, they would write him out of the family trust as well as their wills.

What did he have to do to not disappoint them this time?

He had to produce grandchildren.

Sometimes it was just too much pressure to be an only child. Although he'd enjoyed a childhood full of luxury, at the present he would give anything to have had a female sibling who was popping a grandchild out every year on schedule. Then maybe the pressure on him would subside. Ah. Wishful thinking.

On the bright side, he **did** have a child to present to them. When he'd explained during one of their long boring dinners in their massive dining hall – not a dining room, a dining hall – he'd piqued their interest when he casually mentioned that he was already a father.

Both his parents had stopped eating, put down their silver utensils, and gave him their full attention. It was at that precise moment he realized that he might have stumbled upon THE way to reclaim a secure place in the family coffers.

"When? Who? Where?" His parents drilled him with questions.

He explained that when he was in college, he'd had a short tryst with a girl.

"Where is she? Was she from a good family? Why hadn't he told them about her?"

Stan was able to maintain a serene demeanor when all he really wanted to do was roll his eyes and laugh. No, he had to keep it together if he wanted to remain a recipient of his family's money.

First of all, he wasn't sure where she was at the moment. He'd only met her family one time, but they seemed presentable, although not of the same societal stature, of course. And finally, he hadn't told them because he was afraid they would be disappointed in him for fathering a child out of wedlock.

Okay, that last one was a lie. He hadn't told them because, to him, none of it was important. The twit had gone and gotten pregnant and it wasn't his fault she wasn't using contraception. He'd been looking for a short-time girlfriend for some meaningless fun, and she happened to be there.

She'd been so naïve. He knew she thought they would get married and stay together forever. When her father had tracked him down and confronted Stan, he'd been able to weasel out of marriage by explaining to the man that he wasn't even sure if he was the father, since she also "dated" so many other boys on campus.

After that encounter, he didn't see her again. When he'd come back for the next semester, she apparently had dropped out, which at the time seemed like good luck for him.

When his phone chirped again, he figured it was time to listen to his mother's message.

"Stanley, this is your mother. Please call me back. Our attorney received back a countersuit from the supposedly very poor mother of your son. Apparently, she was able somehow to hire an attorney who certainly appears to know what she's doing. This won't be as simple as we first thought."

Stanly gritted his teeth as he erased the message. He'd call her back later.

Instead of spending the day as he'd planned, on the yacht of a fellow he'd recently met, he'd have to track down Wren again and find out who this attorney of hers was.

No, it was not the day he'd planned.

And he wasn't happy about it. In fact, it put him in a very bad mood that he needed to take out on someone else. And he knew just who it would be.

Chapter Twenty-Four

When Wren didn't answer her door, Stanley fumed. Where was she anyway? Wasn't the library closed for repairs? Where could she possibly be?

He returned to his car to make further plans.

First, he decided he would drive past the library. Perhaps she was there for some reason or another.

If he couldn't' find her there, then he would stop at the office of the woman's attorney, which his mother had texted to him with an admonishment to *Fix this*! Maybe he'd even demand to be given Wren's phone number, since it was the one thing the private detective had been unable to uncover for whatever reason.

Hidden from Stan was the data that the PI had seen the woman with her young son several weeks ago and had followed them around. By the time the PI pulled away from the curb down the street from the apartment they'd just entered, there was no way he was going to make this easy for the Auerbach's. He'd seen over the years how much damage they'd done to anyone who'd gotten in their way. And this woman and her child weren't the conniving parties he'd been told they were. No. Their innocence touched everything about them.

After this assignment, he was going to quit doing work for them. He'd had it and he didn't care how much they paid him.

Stanley used his GPS to find the library in town.

He pulled up in front of it and looked around.

What a ridiculously humble building. Instead of doing whatever it was they were going to do to it, they should just raze it and build something entirely new and modern. It looked like it had been built in the last century.

Actually, Stanley wasn't far off. The Largo Bay Library had started out as the home of one of the founding families almost two hundred years ago. It had slowly grown along with the town and was now having to meet current city codes that hadn't been there when it was first built.

Not seeing anyone or anything that could help his quest, Stanley punched in the address his mother had texted to him.

When it popped up as the Public Defender's Office, it threw him off for a moment. This was a private suit his parents had launched. It had not been brought by any district attorney. Although, if they'd been able to pull off that stunt, they would have.

Okay. Whatever.

He headed to the address, having to drive down the main street to get there. The quaintness of it all made him shudder. To be sure, he'd need to call up his new friend and see if they could reschedule the yacht excursion soon.

He parked in the handicapped spot right next to the front walkway. Then, he pulled out the placard that made his parking there legal and hung it from the rearview mirror. As usual, he checked in the mirror to make sure he looked good and exited the car.

The building held several government offices, according to a large sign on the wall that listed the offices in alphabetical order. He didn't bother looking it up for himself. Instead, he walked over to the gray-haired lady sitting at the reception desk and asked which floor the Public Defender's Office was on.

Instead of answering his question, she smiled and asked for the name of the person he wanted to see. She was trying to be helpful. Since the Public Defender's Office covered two floors of the building, she was going to give him specific directions to help him get there sooner.

He became instantly irritated with the woman and leaned over the desk in order to get in her face.

"Just tell me the floor number. Stop trying to make this complicated."

The smile left the woman's face only to be replaced by a stern look that would have (and had in the past) withered the person it was directly upon.

"Fourth floor." She pursed her lips in condemnation at the rude man.

"There now, that wasn't so difficult, was it?" Stanley shot her a plastic smile while he praised her like he would a dog who'd just completed a command. Of course, he'd never get close to any dog, but that's beside the point.

She followed his path to the elevators and watched him get in and the doors closed behind him.

Then she called her friend at the police station.

"Hi, Annie! It's me. Some bigshot guy just parked his car in our handicapped spot. From here it looks like he has a placard, but I am positive he is not handicapped. Can you have one of the officers cruise past and take a look?"

Well, Annie was more than happy to do the woman's bidding since they were bridge partners at the senior citizen center on Thursday nights.

Stanley got off on the fourth floor and looked around. There were lots of desks, but no apparent reception area. He stood there for a moment then stopped the first person who walked past him.

"Excuse me, but I'm looking for a..." He glanced down at his mother's text. "A Ms. Charlotte McGannon?"

"Next floor up." The man continued walking.

Stanley glared at the man for his rudeness and lack of assistance. If the man had truly been a public servant, he should have escorted him to the woman's office himself.

He turned around and headed back to the elevators. He punched the button but apparently the elevator was being held on one of the floors for something, so he looked around for the stairwell door.

Finding it, he took the stairs up to the next floor. He opened the stairwell door and immediately saw the reason the elevator wasn't working. There was a UPS guy unloading what looked to be a large number of bankers boxes. He'd put a wedge in the door so he could unload everything in one take.

Stanley sniffed with disdain at the worker and the trouble the man had caused him before looking around the large open area in front of him. There were desks everywhere with cubicle dividers between them. Again, no reception desk.

He started to walk over to one of the closer cubicles to ask someone but spotted enclosed offices along the walls and changed his direction.

There were names on each door, so he just continued to walk around the room, finally arriving at a door with the woman's name on it.

Looking through the large plate glass window, he could see no one was there. The light wasn't on and the desk looked tidied up, as though she'd already left for the day.

This inability to get anywhere with his mother's demand was starting to grate on him. Now what? He glanced over at a large clock on the wall next to the elevator and saw it was lunchtime, which might explain why there seemed to be no one there.

He headed over to the stairwell exit since the UPS guy seemed to now be loading up the elevator with more boxes. It didn't occur to Stanley that the guy had chosen this particular time to deliver because he already knew the majority of the staff for that floor had already left for lunch and he wouldn't be holding anyone up.

Stanley took the stairs all the way down to the first floor, crossed the large reception area to the front doors and exited.

He'd gotten out his key fob to start the A/C in the car but hesitated when he noticed the police officer standing next to his car. He approached the woman and asked her what she was doing.

Shea answered with her own question. "Is this your vehicle, Sir?" She already had her hand on her ticket pad to write him a ticket.

"Yes it is. Is there a problem?" Stanley tried his best to look sincerely puzzled.

"It depends. Could I please see your license and registration, Sir?"

He suppressed his irritation and handed her his license from his wallet.

"I need to open the car to get my registration."

"That will be fine." Shea calmly stood there, waiting like she had all the time in the world. She saw his name on the license and instantly knew who this man was. He was the guy trying to harm Dom's new girlfriend.

"Here you are." Stanley handed over the registration slip.

"Thank you." She took the paper and headed back to her police car to run him.

He stood outside his car and waited. Why was she taking so long?

Finally, she came back and handed him his license and registration paper.

"Sir, is the handicapped placard hanging from your mirror for your use? Are you the legal owner of it?"

Stanley didn't know if there was any way she could, or already had, looked up the person who it had been issued to; namely his grandmother who'd died last year. When he was at the wake held at the woman's house after the burial service, he'd seen it hanging from her car's rearview mirror and taken it with him. She didn't have any need for it.

He decided that this time, it just might be expeditious to tell the truth.

He put on a fake embarrassment, as though she'd caught him, and said, "No, Ma'am. It is my grandmother's."

"You do know you are not legally allowed to use it to park in handicapped parking spaces, don't you?"

"Well, I didn't know for sure, but I imagine that would be correct."

Shea knew he was putting her on, but she stayed levelheaded and continued. "Sir, I'm going to have to write you a ticket for this infraction."

"Oh! Can't you just give me a warning and let me off since I didn't actually know I couldn't do this sort of thing?"

She bit back the retort she was going to give him and settled for, "No, Sir. I can't. You took the one and only parking spot available for anyone who is handicapped to use. Wouldn't you think a public services building like this one would have a few people who might need the parking space?"

He paused. Maybe the fine wouldn't be that big. He'd accept the ticket and then get on with his day.

"Thank you for explaining that to me. I understand and will pay the fine."

She finished filling out the form and tore off his copy of it and handed it to him. He smiled at her and folded the thing, putting it in his back pocket. He started to get into the car when Shea spoke up again.

"And since your grandmother is now deceased, you'll have no need to keep the placard. I'll take it with me." She hadn't actually known the woman had passed away, but she took a chance her hunch was right.

Stanley could barely keep his anger in check when he jerked the card off the mirror and practically threw it at Shea.

All she did in response was to catch the thing and add, "Have a nice day, Sir." She turned back to her vehicle and sat in the driver's seat, waiting to see if he'd peel out of the parking lot, at which point if he did, she was going to pull him over and write another ticket.

He held it together long enough to drive back to his hotel without blowing through any stop signs or red lights or going above the speed limit of the horrid tiny town.

After he'd left the parking lot, Shea got out of her vehicle and waved at the short older woman who was watching from the building's front window.

The woman smiled and waved back. Her only thought being, *that ticket is a five hundred dollar fine in Largo Bay.*

Chapter Twenty-Five

Wren couldn't believe what the Largo Bay Fire Department Chief was saying, so she asked him to repeat himself.

"Ms. Johnson, I am more than happy to say it again. We have the funding to begin work on the library. I've already contacted the vendors we're using and I will meet everyone at the library on Friday around noon. You are more than welcome to be there also."

Wren's squeal of delight over the phone line was all the answer he needed.

"Excellent! We'll see you there."

Wren ended the call after profusely thanking the man and turned toward Caleb who'd been standing there silently, knowing it was an important call that couldn't be interrupted.

"We did it! We have the funding for the library repairs!"

Caleb ran over to his mom and gave her a huge hug. She hugged him back until he couldn't breathe and laughing, pushed away from her.

"Does this mean we can see Dom now?"

All the joy drained from Wren while she struggled with how to answer her son's innocent question. All he'd known was that there was a problem with the library and his mom couldn't work there right now and Dom had something to do with it.

"Mom?" His voice was much smaller now. "Are you okay?"

The care and empathy coming from her young son gave Wren the strength she needed at the moment.

"Sorry about that! I'm good." Wren was speaking the truth. The fact her son was becoming such a good person filled her with joy. "What do you want for dinner?"

"Can we have fish sticks?" That, along with mashed potatoes, was one of Caleb's favorite meals. If she let him, Wren knew she could serve that particular meal every evening for every dinner and he'd be happy about it.

"You got it. Do you want to help make it tonight?" Usually, she sent him off to go do something in the other room when she cooked, but tonight she thought it might be a good idea to start involving him in their day-to-day chores.

Caleb's eyes grew wide with her offer. "Yes! Can I do the potatoes?"

"You bet."

It turned out to be an exceptionally nice evening for both of them. Caleb figured he'd ask his mom about Dom tomorrow instead.

The fire chief hung up his desk phone and looked across at Dom who'd been sitting there patiently throughout the man's conversation with Wren.

"I assume you'll be there at the meeting on Friday?"

Dom was already nodding yes before the man had finished his question. There was no way he was going to pass up the opportunity to be close to Wren, even if it was in a professional capacity.

He missed her. And he missed her son. The more she pushed Dom away from her and Caleb, the more he wanted to be with them; protect them; take care of them; like a husband and father would.

He thanked his boss for making the call then left the fire station to go have dinner with his dad, Shea, Luca, and Zach. They were going to go over some of the plans for the upcoming benefit concert.

Dom had promised his dad he'd stop by *The Casablanca* and pick up the meal Erin had prepared for them that evening.

Max had ordered a new dish of Erin's. It was a casserole with ground beef, bell peppers, Vidalia onions, and a mushroom sauce with spices. On top of the dish, Erin added a layer of sauteed mushrooms and shredded cheese before putting it in the oven. Once it came out, she then sprinkled crispy French fried onions on top of the whole thing.

Something about the combination of flavors and textures was very satisfying. It was quickly becoming Max's favorite comfort food.

Dom arrived at the restaurant and before he could even get out of his truck, Paul came out of the restaurant's front door with two large white paper bags in his arms.

"Hey! This is great! Practically door to door service!" Dom took the bags and placed them in the insulated box he kept in the back of his truck for food. It handled both hot and cold items very nicely.

"Too bad you won't get a delivery boy tip from Max." Paul joked.

"No, that's true. BUT! I will get a plateful of this wonderful new recipe from Erin!"

"And as usual, there is a side salad, bread, and dessert included." Paul mentioned.

"I hope the family discount isn't eating a hole in the budget! We all buy a lot of food from you guys."

"Yep. And Erin and I both love it, so keep on using the discount." Paul patted the top of Dom's truck in a "bye" gesture as Dom backed out of the parking space.

The men quickly waved at each other, then went back to their respective schedules.

Which for Paul included a late night beach walk with Erin after they closed the restaurant.

Across town, Char and Bobby were setting the table for an etouffee that his housekeeper had left in the oven for them.

Bobby put on the kitchen mitts and pulled the divinely fragrant food out of the oven just as Char set out the breadbasket and a crock of spiced butter.

Setting the dish on the iron trivet in the center of the table, he slipped off the mitts and held Char's chair out for her to take a seat.

As she slid into the seat, her warm eyes caressed his face.

He gently pushed the chair in then leaned down to kiss her before taking his own seat.

That meal, and what followed afterwards, was a perfect evening for both of them.

The entire expanded McGannon clan enjoyed a restful respite from the recent worries that had been plaguing their lives.

If only the calmness could last just a few more days.

Chapter Twenty-Six

Wren debated about what to wear that Friday to the library meeting. She'd dropped off Caleb at school that morning with his signed permission slip in hand for him to go to the beach with his class. They were being rewarded with the beach trip because they'd all reached their reading targets the previous week.

And now, she was standing in front of her open closet and not liking anything she saw. She hadn't realized just how much her wardrobe had changed after she'd had Caleb. She used to wear fitted jean, slacks, and shorts with cute little tops with cap sleeves and pretty colors.

Now, everything looked like "mom" clothes. Practical. Ordinary. No bright colors. And most of the items were one size too large.

She mentally scolded herself for even caring about how she looked today. Oh, sure, Dom might be there, that shouldn't have anything to do with how she dressed.

After a very large eyeroll at herself, she picked out an old soft pair of jeans and the one pink tee shirt she owned. At least the soft shade went nicely with her skin and eyes.

She didn't want to look like she was trying to look good, because she knew Dom would read that like an invitation.

Which it was.

If she was being honest with herself.

And for once she was.

She gave herself the okay to mess – a little bit – with her hair and add a smidge more eye makeup. If the man took it as an invitation … oh heck, she'd think about that later.

She pulled up to the library and saw several construction type trucks sitting at the curb. There was also a fire station truck and a small car. Wren peered closer. Was that Mrs. Abbott's car?

She found a parking spot and quickly gathered her things before heading to the library's large front door which had already been unlocked and left open. Probably to let in some air after it had been closed for so long, Wren thought to herself.

She took a deep breath and called out a greeting to the people gathered around a couple of tables that had been pushed together. As she got closer she could see it was covered with papers, blueprints, notepads, and assorted pens and pencils.

Everyone was standing except for Mrs. Abbott who'd taken a seat right next to Dom.

"Hello, Wren! Come over here." Mrs. Abbott seemed pleased with herself about something.

Wren reached the woman's chair and whispered, "Am I late? I thought the meeting was for noon."

"Oh! I guess you didn't get the message. We moved it up to eleven so we could all see what everyone had come up with."

"For what? Aren't the repairs just regular average repairs?"

"Not anymore they're not." Dom's deep voice whispered across the short space between them.

She looked up into his eyes and instantly felt enveloped by the warmth and caring she found in them. At that moment all she wanted to do was wrap her arms around his waist while he held her. The upset she'd been hanging onto seemed so small and insignificant right now.

Mrs. Abbott finally nudged her gently before saying, "Wren. They're going to do a little more during the time the library is closed. They want your permission to carry forward with the project. Could you please look at what they've brought to present?"

Wren's attention went to all the men standing around the makeshift worktable.

They all sent smiles or outright grins in her direction as her eyes travelled around the group.

"Wow. I'm afraid I'm a little bit behind you. Please tell me what's happening."

The fire chief spoke up first. "It turns out the fundraising we've been doing has produced much more income than we'd anticipated. And with the singer Luca Napier also offering to hold a benefit concert on behalf of the library, we now have enough for a few more projects."

"Like what?" Wren was still trying to grapple with the fact that all these people were there to help. That the townspeople had given more than they'd hoped for just made her head spin.

"My company would like to upgrade the air conditioning and ducting for the building."

"We want to expand the children's corner out several feet in all directions to give you more room for the programs Mrs. Abbott said you wanted to implement."

"Painting this beautiful building would be our absolute pleasure."

"We've already ordered the upgraded refrigerator and stove for the staff's break room."

At this point, all Wren could do was try to hold back her happy tears at all of the men's offers for the library. It was almost beyond comprehension.

Mrs. Abbott spoke up, "And the Women's' Guild is donating a huge list of bestselling books."

"How huge?" The first thing that had come to Wren's mind was that there wasn't enough book shelving to handle all of it.

As if reading her concerns, another man who hadn't spoken yet stated, "Ms. Johnson. My company will be adding an addition to the library. We already have the permits pulled. I think you'll like what we've come up with."

As she dissolved into tears at the emotion that overwhelmed her. It was almost too much to bear. She covered her face with her hands and stood there sobbing until a pair of strong arms wrapped around her and she could bury her face in the tee shirt that covered a chest she recognized.

Dom smiled and held her while she let it all out. The men silently agreed to head over toward the areas they would be restoring and quietly talked amongst themselves. This was a private moment they all could understand.

But not Mrs. Abbott. She sat there in her chair with a contented look on her face as though she'd planned the whole thing.

Maybe she had.

Chapter Twenty-Seven

"Mother, I told you the woman wasn't available to speak with." Stanley was still in a snit from yesterday's series of unfortunate incidents. It wasn't his fault the lawyer couldn't be found. He was getting tired of being blamed for everything that went wrong.

"Yes, Stanley. I heard you the first time." Even her voice had a backbone of steel in it. "What I need you to do is to make her see you. Do I need to come down there and do it myself?"

Just the thought of that possibility made his skin crawl.

"No. I'll do it."

"Today, Stanley."

"Yes, Mother. Today."

He waited until she'd ended the call and then he threw his phone across the hotel room in a rage. All he wanted to do was smash everything around him. The gilded mirrors, the expensive furniture, the silk draperies – everything!

It took the very last shred of control he had to not mess up the place. All that would bring in the long run was more trouble.

He finally calmed down enough to go retrieve his phone from in front of the couch where it had landed on the thick carpet.

It was in pristine condition.

He couldn't even damage a phone properly.

Maybe his mother was right. Maybe he wasn't worth much at all.

Char looked up from the papers on her desk and finally noticed the man standing in her doorway. How long had he been standing there, observing her? She didn't recognize him, but he was sure sending out some major conflicting vibes. A warning bell went off inside her.

She glanced around the office, then at the clock on her desk. It was only a few minutes after six, but it looked like everyone else had already cleared out for the coming weekend.

She folded her hands on top of her desk and asked, "May I help you?"

"I believe you may." Stanley had waited in the stairwell for almost an hour, hoping against hope everyone would leave except for her. When he quietly opened the door after he'd heard the elevator ping for the last time, he saw the light was still on in her office. Maybe his luck was changing after all.

He strolled across Char's office and took a chair across the desk from her. He sat back and crossed one leg over the other in a casual motion. He finished by smoothing his pantleg crease across the knee before finally looking up at her.

His eyes were the coldest eyes she'd ever seen.

Although she remained cool and collected on the outside, her mind was frantically searching for a way out of the situation.

BEAUTY AND THE BOOKS

She casually leaned down next to her chair where she'd left her purse and phone when she'd finally gotten back to the office.

"Good. What can I do for you, Mr. ...?" She smiled as she kept her eyes locked on him and reached into the purse and found her phone immediately.

"My name is Stanley Auerbach, but I think you already know that don't you Ms. McGannon?"

Her eyes widened in feigned confusion as she answered, "I'm afraid I don't know who you are, Sir." Then she blatantly opened her desk's center drawer as though looking for a pen or something to write with while she surreptitiously hit the speed dial button for 911.

"Close the drawer, Ms. McGannon. I'm not sure what you're looking for but you won't need it for our conversation."

The fact she was even able to breathe, much less pretend casualness, surprised Char. "Oh! Okay." She slowly shut the drawer as if it meant nothing to her.

She once again rested both hands on top of her desk and waited for the man to continue.

"I'm sure I'm right in saying you are the attorney who is representing Ms. Wren Johnson."

When she didn't even blink, he added, "The mother of my son."

Char could only pray the 911 operator could hear what was going on. But to make sure, she answered him. "Yes. I am Charlotte McGannon, the attorney for Ms. Johnson. Mr. Auerbach, what are you doing in my office at this hour of the day? As you can see, everyone else has headed home for the weekend and I'm here all alone."

"Yes. That is true. You are all alone. Which suits me just fine. I want your full attention on what I'm about to instruct you to do, regarding my son."

"Should I be taking notes?" Char tried to keep the edge of anger that was starting to boil up inside of her at the man's clearly intended threats.

When he saw her anger, he threw his head back and laughed. "I was told you might have some fire in you." Then he relaxed back into the chair. "No. No notes. Nothing in writing. You're an attorney, make mental notes and use them."

"Okay. Go ahead." She didn't dare look down to see if the call to 911 had connected or not. In fact, she hoped she'd actually hit the right button!

"First of all, you will drop the countersuit you filed against my parents."

"Why?" At this point, she was stalling for time in the hope the authorities were already on their way.

"Because you'll lose." Stanley said it with a certainty which led Char to guess his parents had friends in high places.

"What happens if my client refuses to drop the lawsuit?"

"I'm not saying your client has to approve of what you're doing. Just do it."

"But I could lose my license if I do that."

"Your choice. But I imagine you'd rather lose your license than your life."

"What?!" Char was unable to tamp down her surprise at the man's statement."

"I mean it, Char. May I call you Char?" Without waiting for anything from her he added, "Thank you, Char. I'm so glad you understand."

He continued, "Next, you'll advise Wren to surrender all rights to our son."

"You know her, she'll never do that." Char had gone very still in the presence of the evil sitting in front of her.

"It would be such a tragedy if something happened to the woman. Of course, then, being his father, I would be more than happy to have him come live with me."

It was almost too much for Char to take, so she fell back onto her go-to place whenever she felt threatened, sarcastic comments.

"You do know you sound like you're reciting lines from a bad movie right now, don't you?" Char relaxed back into her chair. At least now she felt somewhat in control of herself.

This wasn't how he wanted her to feel right now. He wanted her to be afraid and willing to do whatever he told her to do. So, he surged to his feet, leaned across the desk, and put his face right in front of hers.

"Don't think for a moment that you can somehow thwart my desires in this instance."

Well, that just about did Char in. And not in a pro-survival way. Nope, not in the least. At first she tried to choke back her laughter. She thought she'd succeeded but couldn't hold everything back, so as her eyes started to water, her breath came out in little uneven puffs.

Of course, he thought she was starting to cave in under his assault.

Nope. When she couldn't help herself any longer, she threw out her arms to the sides and started braying. "Did you hear yourself? 'Thwart my desires!!!'" Then she held her sides as her ribs started to burn from the onslaught of glee she just couldn't halt.

Well, of course, Stanley didn't know how to handle the woman. Either he charmed them or threatened them. Up until now, both those tactics had worked.

But here he was, sitting across from this obviously crazy woman and he had no idea how to get her attention.

He was vacillating between kidnapping her or running out of the building to save his own life when he heard the ping of the elevator as its doors opened across the room from them.

Several officers rushed toward him as he put his hands and arms up covering his head to protect himself.

The worst part about his arrest was the fact they all laughed at him.

He couldn't even be a good criminal.

He'd never felt so low in his life.

Chapter Twenty-Eight

Later that night, Char recounted her adventure, as she'd dubbed it, for the second time, since Shea and Luca had now joined everyone who'd gathered at Max's place.

The only person missing was Dom. He was still over at Wren's place and no one wanted to interrupt if they were coming to any sort of agreement.

"That was really smart, calling 911 like you did." Shea's admiration for her sister's fast thinking was evident.

"Well, that's what you'd always told me to do if I needed help. Call 911. It was because of your insistence that I'd put it on speed dial."

"I'm so happy it helped tonight."

"We all are." Max added to the conversation.

When they'd all quieted down with their own thoughts, Max asked, "Anyone hungry?"

Of course, being McGannons, they all were.

"Let's raid the fridge!" Erin was already out of her seat and heading into the kitchen.

Caleb was showing Dom the newest space city he and Wylie had constructed. Of course, Dom acknowledged it all with enthusiasm.

Wren was in the kitchen fixing them a bite to eat.

She shook her head at her own stubbornness. Right now, the fact he hadn't told her about how the library was going to have to close didn't seem like that big of a deal. After all, when he realized they would need to find their own funding, he'd gone out of his way to make it happen.

She just wished it didn't have to be a calendar of attractive male firefighters, including Dom, with their shirts off. Swear to goodness, if the photographer has them put oil on their chests and biceps, that would be it! She would be done with the whole thing.

Wren had worked herself back into being upset when Dom stuck his head in the kitchen and immediately became the recipient of her glare.

"Uh oh." He knew he was in trouble, but not for what or how much. He swallowed a sigh. And here everything had been going so well.

"Can I help with anything?"

"No. I think you've done enough." Wren stirred the pot of mac 'n cheese with a vengeance.

He decided to take his life in his hands and slowly walk over to where Wren was. When he got there he gently removed the long spoon from her hand and set it down on the spoon holder located next to the stove top.

When she hadn't moved, he put his hands on her shoulders and turned her around so she faced him.

"Wren?" He tried to get her to look at him, but she wouldn't. "What happened?"

"Nothing." He almost didn't hear her answer.

He tried again. His voice was a little stronger this time. "Wren?"

Now, she looked into his eyes while hers brimmed with unshed tears. "I don't want to tell you."

"Well, in that case, don't you think you should? If we're going to be honest with each other from now on, this would be a good place to start."

If she told him about her worries, she'd be giving him ammunition against her.

How? She didn't really know.

All she knew was that at this moment, she felt very vulnerable. And she didn't like the feeling.

On the other hand, if she didn't tell him about her concerns, she would be the one to first break their newfound trust with each other.

This was so frustrating!

Come on, Wren. Choose. Pick one. You'll feel better, even if it's the wrong choice. Sitting in the middle and going back and forth is killing you.

She lowered her eyes and took in a breath to speak.

Just then the pot boiled over, so she and Dom worked together to get things under control. He moved the pot off the burner. She turned the burner off. They both grabbed paper towels and mopped the mess off the stovetop.

When they finished, instead of resuming their conversation, Wren put her hand on his chest and said, "I'm fine, Dom. I'm fine."

Then she got three bowls down from the cupboard and announced, "Dinner's ready!"

She heard Caleb run down the hallway to wash his hands even before she had to remind him. She gave Dom credit for that, since he'd explained to the boy how many germs could possibly get inside his stomach from dirty hands and that then he'd probably throw up, maybe even for a couple of days!

Wren admired the method. In fact, she wished she'd come up with it!

Their supper was mainly silent as they all ate their fill. There was a calmness that surrounded Wren, having Caleb sit across from her and Dom sitting at the end of the table. It was almost like a family, which seemed to make everyone happy.

After finishing their food, the three of them cleaned up the kitchen, washed the dishes, dried them, and put everything away in record time. They made a good team.

When Caleb asked Dom if he'd read to him, it almost melted Wren's heart. She watched as the two of them sat side by side, Dom reading the story and Caleb taking it all in.

It was almost too perfect.

Wren didn't know why she felt that way, only that most things in her life hadn't turned out the way she'd wanted them to.

Yet maybe – just maybe – this time it might.

Wren finished tucking Caleb into bed and kissed him goodnight.

Before she left he asked her, "Mom? Can Dom come back tomorrow?"

The wistfulness in her son's question caught her off guard. Yes, she'd known he was fond of the man. But now, he was apparently feeling something closer, something stronger with the relationship.

It made her nervous, but she answered, "Of course he can." When she saw Caleb's smile, she got up and headed for the door. She turned around to blow a kiss to her son, but he'd already closed his eyes. She quietly turned off the light switch and closed the door.

When she got back out to the living room, Dom had already gathered up his stuff and was waiting for her.

"I'm going to take off. Tomorrow starts early for me."

Wren was aware of a feeling of disappointment that he was already leaving, which she expected, but was still surprised by it. She sighed and knew she had to make some firm decisions about this man standing in front of her. And she had to make them soon.

"Thank you for coming with me after the library meeting." Then she added, "Caleb was so happy to see you again."

"I was happy to see him again, too." She expected Dom to say more after that but instead he turned to the door and opened it.

He looked back over his shoulder and said, "I'll see you later." She nodded back. "Yep. We'll see you later."

That seemed to be all he was looking for. He smiled and went out the door, shutting it quietly behind him.

She went over and locked the door, included putting on the chain she'd installed.

She smiled when she heard from the other side of the door, "Good girl."

Chapter Twenty-Nine

Luca and Shea were out shopping for an engagement ring. He hadn't really planned for his marriage proposal to her. He'd just been moved in the moment, so hadn't had a ring ready for her at the time.

He wanted to get her something bigger than she wanted. And he wanted to get it for her before he had to leave for New York again.

She tried explaining to him that she felt more comfortable with a smaller stone.

Luca thought all women liked jewelry. In fact, the bigger the better as far as he understood.

Yet, here was Shea claiming she didn't want anything fancy.

She explained to him how it might get in her way on the job. It took him a moment to catch on.

She finally had to add, "If I'm taking down a suspect, I don't want him to be able to use the ring against me."

"How would he do that?" Luca wasn't enjoying this conversation about potential harm coming to his woman.

"Why do you think I keep my hair pinned to my head so tightly? It's so someone can't grab it and pull me down to the ground. A flashy diamond ring would be the first thing a criminal would want to take from me."

The thought of Shea having to fight a man made Luca's stomach twist. If he'd been thinking straight he wouldn't have said the next thing he did.

"I really want you to quit your job. I am able to support both of us now."

Shea just stared at him. Was that what he thought was important? That they'd get married and she'd just quit her job helping people? This was not a side to Luca that she recognized at all.

However, she didn't want to create a scene in public. Everyone around her knew who she was. She figured she'd fight this particular fight another day.

"You know what? I'm suddenly starving." She put her hand through his arm. "Take me to lunch?" She planted a kiss on his cheek and batted her eyes at him.

He didn't understand the sudden change in Shea's demeanor, but he was happy to take her to lunch if that was what she wanted. Heck, he'd do anything she asked.

Marlene had just finished updating her window display when she heard the shop's doorbell chime as someone came in.

She backed out of the area, keeping her head ducked down so she didn't bang her head on the top of the small door she used to access the display area.

Max stood there, watching the woman back out of the short door. He knew he should look away and give her some privacy, but he couldn't help noticing she had the cutest backside he'd seen in a long time.

She finally stood up straight and turned around before he could shift his eyes away. She noticed where he'd been looking and found the thought made her feel better than she'd been feeling all week. Maybe she wasn't too old for men to notice her!

"Hi, Max! Did your daughter like her birthday gift?"

He finally found his tongue and was able to answer. "Yes. I was surprised but she really liked it!" Then he added, "Thank you, Marlene for your suggestion."

When she glanced at his head, he realized he'd kept on his hat. It was an old cowboy hat the Largo Bay City Council had presented to him when he'd caught the drug trafficker. He'd worn it ever since. He knew he should probably get a new one, but there really was no reason to buy another cowboy hat since he was not a cowboy, nor did he ride a horse.

And since he didn't want to wear a regulation cap, he avoided it by keeping on wearing the cowboy hat.

He swiftly swiped the hat off his head and held it between his hands.

"Sorry 'bout that."

Marlene noticed his wry smile and realized all the man needed was a horse standing behind him and he could be the poster boy for "hot older cowboy." Maybe like one of the ones she saw on the covers of some of her favorite books.

"Do you ride?" She nodded at the hat.

"Oh! Um. No." Max couldn't help stumbling around his words. He was still embarrassed because he knew she'd caught him checking her out. "I mean I can ride. I know how to ride. I just ... don't."

Brilliant Max, brilliant.

He stood there silently, so Marlene carried on with the conversation. His humility was another point scored for him. She didn't enjoy being around arrogant guys. Been there, done that.

"Do you need another gift for someone?"

"What?" Max looked confused for a moment. "No, I don't think so." He chuckled. "Unless I've forgotten someone's birthday or something."

"Okay." Marlene couldn't stop the smile from happening. "Then, why are you here?"

"Why am I here?"

"Hm-mmm." She waited for his answer.

"Honestly?" He glanced at her.

"That's how I prefer it." She stood there with her hands on her hips, waiting for him to continue.

"I guess I just wanted to see you." Then he added. "You know, see how the shop was doing and how Largo Bay was treating you."

"Just fine. Thank you for asking." Marlene had the sneaking suspicion he was holding something back but didn't press him for more.

"Well! Good. In that case I'll just be going." Max didn't want to leave, but he couldn't have told anyone why. Maybe he was just lonely for some conversation with a female that wasn't family.

As though picking up on his thought, Marlene gently asked, "Would you like some coffee? I just made a pot and can't possibly drink it all myself."

Max's face relaxed. In fact, his whole body relaxed.

"I'd love a cup."

Chapter Thirty

It was finally the night of the concert and Luca was pumped. Apparently, Zach had been able to get a couple of the local TV stations to cover the event, which brought even more people in, since the reporters had been promoting it during their various segments.

The permits were posted backstage, the light and sound crew were all set up, the stage had been assembled since earlier in the week.

The park where the stage was now located was cordoned off during the day today and the ticket booths were doing a booming business.

Luca was in the RV they'd rented as his dressing room and right now it was just him and Shea sitting around, waiting. Zach was out front making sure everything was running the way it should.

"I hope we bring in plenty for the library's expansion." Luca loved the idea of helping Largo Bay in a big way, since the town had helped him get where he was now. It had given him a place to heal from the betrayal of his previous agent, as well as his ex-girlfriend/manager.

He was happy for Theresa now, since it looked like she was turning her life around. He guessed some time in jail could do that to anyone. As for Marty, he was under indictment in New York for money laundering, and various other crimes Luca had no idea the man had done. Somehow, he didn't hold out much hope for Marty's future.

Shea smiled at him. He looked like an excited kid at the moment. She truly loved the fact that he liked to help so much. Now if she could just get him to realize she didn't want to stop working. However, tonight was neither the time nor the place to get into it. No. Tonight was a great night for Largo Bay and she was glad to help in any way she could.

Right now, she'd been hired by Zach to be Luca's bodyguard. It wasn't that he needed protection, it was more for show. At least that was what Zach said. Either way, she'd be on high alert when they were outside.

"How about a kiss for good luck!" Luca stood up and held out his arms to Shea. She smiled as he pulled her close. When his lips touched hers, everything within her just melted. The kiss was just starting to get more serious when Zach threw open the RV door and climbed inside.

"Oops! Sorry about that!"

They'd jumped apart when they heard the door open. But after seeing it was Zach, Luca moved forward and put his hand on Shea's face before giving her a small kiss.

"Just getting a good luck kiss from the lady." Luca smiled at his friend, who just grinned back.

"I think that's an excellent idea. Maybe even a tradition to start!" Zach stood there for a moment before adding, "It's time! Ready to rock 'n roll?"

"I'm ready. Let's go."

Shea checked to make sure she had everything she needed and then preceded Luca down the RV steps. She kept an eye out as they crossed to the back of the stage where the stage manager was waiting for them.

The man greeted them and ushered them up to the wings to wait for the cue for Luca to enter the stage.

Shea could feel butterflies of excitement start; something she had not expected.

Looking around at all the gadgets and equipment, she vowed to understand all of it, even if only to impress Luca. However, it was mainly to know for future events what belonged and what didn't. She figured it would help her when she traveled on Luca's tours with him.

Yes, she'd finally made the decision she would go on his tours, as his main bodyguard, and work the rest of the time at the Largo Bay PD when they were home. She hadn't told him yet. But she would after tonight.

Dom had gotten there early and saved seats for everyone else in the family as well as Wren and Caleb, his friend, Wylie, and the boy's parents.

The place was packed! Which meant a ton of tickets had been sold. Even when Zach tried to give them all comp tickets, they refused and insisted on paying. After all, it was their library that was being helped.

The chairs were all taken and now there was standing room only. Or sitting if you had brought your own beach chair or even a towel.

He was craning his neck looking for any of them when he spotted Wren looking around. She knew he was waiting for her, so he waved and shouted to her. Caleb was the one who heard his voice in the crowd and spotted him up front. Caleb ran toward him and jumped up and down in front of him.

"Dom! This is great! Wylie should be here pretty soon. Which are our chairs?"

Dom pointed out two from the row he'd saved. He had the boys situated between their parents so they wouldn't be able to run off without being seen. Sure, it was Largo Bay but it was never safe for a child to run off in any crowd.

Dom watched as Wren caught up with her son.

But instead of the cautioning he figured the kid would get, she was grinning and looking around at everything, just as excited as Caleb.

Plus, she had on a new blouse and shorts, which looked just right on her. Not too much like some women, but it was no longer an outfit trying to hide her body, either. In fact, Dom approved very much.

The fun part was seeing her expression as she realized he liked what she was wearing. A little bit shy with just a dash of flirt. It wasn't as if he didn't know she'd put a lot of time into figuring out what to wear to tonight's event. She'd even done something to her hair and was definitely wearing more eye makeup than usual.

He nodded at her with a grin and she curtsied an acknowledgement of his perusal and masculine approval.

Caleb shouted to his friend. He'd been standing on his chair looking for him. Wylie and his parents made it to the front and found their seats.

Quickly after that everyone else showed up. They only had about ten minutes before the show started, so Wylie's dad took the boys to go pick up some hot dogs, popcorn, and sodas after taking everyone's order.

That left a little time for Dom and Wren to just sit and talk quietly. The rest of the group gave them some semblance of privacy, as it was obvious the two were only aware of each other.

Finally, the boys arrived back with Wylie's dad and several bags filled with complete junk food, which everyone enjoyed, knowing they'd regret it a little tomorrow.

A microphone was turned on somewhere and a man's voice said, "Ladies and Gentlemen! Please take your seats as the show will start in less than five minutes!"

Applause broke throughout the crowd at the announcement.

Backstage, Luca had been doing some vocal warmups and stretching, making sure he was in top form for this performance. It was going to be an hour long set with an extra fifteen minutes for an encore.

Shea watched him in fascination. And as she watched, she came to realize just how hard he was working for his. It wasn't like when he'd plop down on her couch, pull out his guitar and play for her while she was making them dinner.

No. This was like an athlete warming up before the game. Dedication, intention, and focus all came together in the promise of an extraordinary performance.

And it was.

From the moment Luca walked onto the stage, guitar in hand, it was magical.

For everyone.

First, he charmed them with his humor and humility. Occasionally, someone would shout out something between songs and he'd pay attention and try to answer them when he could. A few times, the audience grew completely quiet as he poured his heart into the song. When it ended they exploded with applause and cheering.

Then it came to the time for him to play his new hit, *Bella*.

But instead of singing, he released the guitar strap and rested the guitar on its stand.

"Would you all mind if I did something kind of different right now?"

"Go ahead!" Someone from the back of the audience shouted out and everyone else laughed and cheered.

"Glad to hear that!" Then he added, "I'll be right back, I promise!"

There was some murmuring among the crowd as they watched him walk off stage. He headed over to where Shea had been standing guard keeping anyone from coming backstage that didn't belong there.

"What are you doing?" She whispered to him as he took one of her hands and turned around, heading back toward the stage with her in tow.

"Luca! Stop!" Shea was trying to pull away but he had a pretty good hold on her. She finally understood she wasn't going to be able to stop him from whatever it was he was about to do.

When they entered the stage, it looked like they were holding hands and not what it really was, him pulling her behind him.

The crowd was mostly quiet while he released her hand and pulled a chair up next to where he'd been standing in front of the mic. Once she was sitting (and didn't look like she was about to disappear backstage) he picked up his guitar and secured the strap over his shoulder. Then he returned to stand next to her chair and in front of the mic.

The crowd heard him say in a soft voice, "Bella, this song is for you."

He started strumming the opening chords and kept his gaze on Shea.

As he sang the song, he sang it straight to her soul. And she got it. Her trembling smile said it all as he moved into the second verse.

By the end of the song beautiful tears filled eyes not only on the stage but throughout the crowd. When Shea sighed in happiness, every woman out there sighed right along with her.

It was a magnificent performance and the local TV crews caught great footage of not only Luca and Shea but also extra scenes with a husband putting his arm around his wife. Another man reached over, picked up his wife's hand and kissed it. There was even a funny scene of a young boy screwing up his face and going "Ewww" when his dad kissed his mom.

All in all, it was one of the most romantic evenings some of those people had experienced in a long time.

When the song ended, it ended to thunderous applause with most of the crowd on their feet in appreciation of Luca's new song.

Yes, it was a wonderful evening. One that had even rekindled some relationships' ashes back into flame.

Chapter Thirty-One

Wren expected Dom to stop by any second now. Last night after the concert he'd walked her and Caleb to her car.

First he'd high-fived Caleb before the boy climbed into the back seat. After he'd helped him buckle in securely, he had whispered, "Is it okay with you if I give your mom a goodbye kiss?"

At first Caleb had just looked at Dom like *why would you want to do something like that?* But then he grinned and covered his eyes with his hands.

"Go ahead."

Dom had ruffled the kid's hair and closed the car's back door.

Then he'd turned to Wren who'd been able to hear everything the two guys had said. Dom had then opened his arms and Wren stepped into their warmth and strength.

The kiss had started out relatively chaste but had then rapidly evolved into something greater than just two sets of lips meeting. It felt to Wren as though Dom was promising without words to take care of her, love her, and be by her side forever.

As for Dom, he hadn't felt this yearning to love, protect, and treasure a woman ever before. His arms had tightened around Wren and she'd moved as close to him as she possibly could. Almost as though she'd wanted to climb into him.

The kiss had deepened into something Dom knew he wanted to take further but couldn't. At least not at that precise moment, so he loosened his hold on her at the same time he gentled the kiss.

She'd leaned back and looked up into his face. She had seen the heat in Dom's eyes and instead of feeling cautious and careful, she'd grinned and said, "Wow."

Dom had replied, "Yes. Wow."

Then he had opened her door and made sure she was all settled before he closed it behind her. He hadn't wanted to let go of her. Not then. Not ever.

And now he was jogging up her front walkway ready to knock on her door. Instead, just as he got there, Wren opened it wide with one of the most dazzling smiles he'd ever seen.

"Hey there." He moved past her into the living room.

"Hey there, yourself." She closed the door and turned to face him.

Dom took one step closer and was about to kiss her when Caleb came bounding loudly down the hallway, so he hesitated.

Wren laughed, knowing her son's grin matched her own.

Yes, they both knew they wanted this wonderful man in their family.

"We're just about to have some breakfast. Although seeing as how it's almost noon I should probably call it brunch. Are you hungry?"

Dom answered, "Yes." Wren knew he wasn't referring to food when his eyes explored her own, as though he was looking for answers.

"I'll ... " Wren cleared her throat which had somehow failed her for a moment. She spoke again, "I'll get started then. How does eggs and pancakes sound?"

Caleb was already jumping up and down at the thought of pancakes.

Dom slowly walked over and stopped right in front of Wren. He placed his hand on her cheek and answered, "It sounds perfect."

Wren knew she was going to need another cup of coffee; her mouth had just gone dry at the heat Dom was directing her way.

"I'll make coffee!" She almost sprinted into the kitchen while trying to hide the blush that was creeping up her neck.

That man made her feel things she had thought she would never feel again

How did he do that, anyway?

Cooking in the kitchen was a little crowded with all three of them working on it, but it was also sort of a bonding for them.

Caleb set the table while Wren prepared the pancake batter.

Dom pulled out the two frying pans they needed and got them heated up and ready for the eggs and batter.

By the time the food was ready they were enjoying the new camaraderie that didn't seem new at all. It felt to Wren like a true family unit.

If she knew what her son was wishing for, she would have agreed with him wholeheartedly.

They'd just finished the meal when someone knocked on Wren's front door. She hadn't been expecting anyone other than Dom, so when he glanced at her with a question, she could only shrug.

"I'll get it." Dom went over to the door and opened it.

"Karla! What are you doing here?" Dom was surprised to see the photographer's assistant standing in Wren's doorway.

By this time, Wren was standing next to Dom and saw the gorgeous young woman who apparently knew Dom.

"You're late! We're doing the final shot at the station. Everyone else is there waiting. Luckily one of them figured out where you might be when I couldn't find you at home."

"Oh! I am so sorry! I forgot all about it!" Dom turned to Wren and gave her a quick kiss on the cheek. "I'll be back soon."

With that rushed goodbye, he was out the door, running to his truck.

Karla looked Wren up and down once, then turned and walked to her car.

Wren stood in the doorway watching them both drive away in the same direction.

What was that and who was Karla?

Caleb was standing next to her and had to tug on her hand to get his mom's attention. "Is Dom coming back?"

When Wren didn't answer and just continued to stare out the door, he tugged harder. This time she looked down at him.

"What?" It took her a moment to come out of whatever it was that had just hit her.

"Is Dom coming back?"

Wren wasn't about to quietly wait around to find out. She leaned over so she was on Caleb's level, plastered the biggest smile on her face she could drum up, and said, "You know what? I totally forgot that I'd made plans for us to go to the waterpark today! Doesn't that sound good?"

Caleb knew something was up with his mom. She was acting so strange. But he **did** like the waterpark. And they hadn't been there in ages.

"Can I call Wylie and see if he can come, too?"

"Sure you can. Why not." Wren straightened back up. "How about you call him and I'll back a bag for us."

Caleb called and got permission for Wylie.

However, his joy lessened a little bit when they were heading out the door and he realized they hadn't cleaned up the kitchen yet, which was something his mom usually insisted on before they left home.

In fact, she didn't seem to have any attention on it at all, she was moving so fast to leave.

Caleb hoped Dom could find them. He had been looking forward to having him around for the whole day.

Chapter Thirty-Two

Wren knew she was acting strangely. She knew she had to calm down and not jump to any conclusions. It was just that she'd never been in a real relationship before and frankly, didn't know what to expect or how to do it.

After they picked up Wylie, they got to the park and found a parking space close to the front entrance.

They grabbed their stuff and headed to the ticket booth. The boys' joy at being at the park put things in a little better perspective for Wren. She knew she could use the break in routine, especially after everything she'd had to contend with over the past several weeks.

They made it to the front of the ticket line. Wren was horrified to find the park had doubled its prices since last year. She knew she had it in the account, but also knew that with the food they'd have to purchase while here, this excursion was going to take a chunk out of Caleb's college savings.

At that precise moment, it struck her that when he got into high school, and maybe even a year or two before that, he'd be able to have a little part-time job and he'd be able to add to the college account.

She looked down at her son while the woman in the booth ran her debit card. She somehow just knew with great certainty that Caleb would be able to do anything he set his mind to.

Her worries over what she was going to end up spending that day just vanished and all of a sudden she felt much lighter.

"Have a swimmingly good time!" The woman's standard company patter made Wren laugh out loud.

"Thank you! We will."

Then she told the boys to stop running and they entered the park, heading for the lockers.

The photo shoot was taking forever! Dom kept thinking it was done but then, "One more shot!"

He was beating himself up for not remembering this. It had been on the calendar for days, but he guessed he'd been thinking about Wren and Caleb so much, that he had honestly just forgotten.

Finally, the photographer announced he had everything he needed and thanked them all for their time.

Dom had already apologized profusely and ended up promising to take kitchen duty for each one of the guys over the next couple of weeks. They seemed pleased with that and he was let off the hook for being late.

He sprinted to his truck and headed over to Wren's place to spend the rest of the day with them.

"Dom!" Karla had shouted out trying to get his attention. He'd left his duffle bag where he'd dropped it earlier when they'd arrived.

He didn't hear her and had sped off.

"That man is going to drive me crazy!" Reluctantly, she grabbed Dom's bag and got in her car, heading over to the address she'd found him at earlier.

She'd known Dom her whole life, following him and her big brother around, bothering them to no end. For a while in her early teens, she'd had a crush on him, which he'd never seemed to notice. Maybe it was that old "don't date your best friend's little sister" thing.

Whatever it was, she grew out of her crush when she met her future husband in high school. Noah was everything Dom was not. To put it plainly, he was a brainiac; smarter than anyone else she'd ever met, and she was drawn to him after meeting him for the first time.

It was funny because none of her friends on the cheerleading squad could figure out why Karla was so single minded when it came to Noah.

Oh, sure, he was cute in a nerdy sort of way, but not what they all considered the perfect guy.

Karla saw something deeper in him. Behind his glasses, there was a look of compassion in his eyes that just pulled her closer to him.

At first, when she approached him after one of the school's football games, he'd seemed distracted and hadn't seemed to pay her much attention. The truth was, he was thrown off when the cutest cheerleader of the bunch walked directly over to him with a wide smile on her face. Her eyes had locked with his and his mind went blank.

That had never happened to him before. He'd always relied on his mind and right at that moment it had flown away completely.

But, as with most love struck teenagers, she'd persisted in her endeavors. Especially after the first time they'd kissed and he'd taken off his glasses. Oh my, those were some gorgeous eyes!

She'd now been happily married to the man right out of high school and they had two kids already. She was hoping to have another one within the next year or so.

But now, she had to return Dom's bag to him, which was taking time away from her family, which she was not happy about.

Dom was standing at Wren's door, knocking for the second time when Karla pulled up behind his truck. She grabbed his pack and strode up the walkway to where he was standing.

"Here, doofus! You left your bag at the shoot." She plonked it down next to where he was standing. She noticed he had a worried look on his face.

"You okay?" Although she was miffed at him right now, he was still her brother's best friend and she wanted to help.

Dom tried knocking one more time, but still no answer.

Where were Wren and Caleb?

Dom didn't think he'd been gone that long, had he?

"Dom? What's up?" Karla could see he was truly concerned about something. Besides, the sooner she helped him, the sooner she could get home to Noah.

She had to nudge him with her elbow twice before he spoke.

"I don't know why they left or where they've gone."

He sounded so forlorn and puzzled.

"Okay. Were they supposed to be waiting here for you?"

Dom looked down and blinked a couple of times before answering, "We didn't say it out loud, but I figured she knew I'd be back as soon as I could."

Karla was starting to realize he really cared about the woman. "Who is she?"

He didn't hesitate this time, "She's the woman I'm going to marry."

Karla was stunned. Largo Bay's most sought-after bachelor was going to get married? She waited for him to say more, but in typical Dom fashion, he didn't.

"Uh. Can you tell me more? I mean, maybe I can help."

"Do you know where they went?" Dom didn't understand what Karla meant.

"How would I know where they went? I don't even know them." She paused. "And, by the way, who is *they*?"

"Oh." Dom was so used to Karla knowing everything because she was like his little sister, he hadn't realized she didn't know who Wren and Caleb were. "Can we sit in my truck? I can run the A/C."

"Sounds good, but I haven't got all day, so you better talk fast."

Dom picked up his bag and she had to almost jog to keep up with him.

They got into Dom's truck and he started it up. The cool air that eventually flowed out of the vents was refreshing for both of them.

He settled back in the set and turned so he was semi-facing Karla and started to speak. He told her about when he'd found Wren by accident and gotten her to the hospital. His eyes lit up when he mentioned how brilliant her son, Caleb, was. And when he spoke of wanting to marry Wren, it was so sincere and heartfelt and romantic it made Karla's eye's mist over at the raw emotion she could feel from him.

By the time he'd finished, she had a couple of questions for him, even though she'd spotted the problem a few sentences ago.

"Where's the boy's father?"

Dom showed his surprise at the question, which seemed to come from out in left field. "He's not in the picture. When she told him she was pregnant, he ended their relationship, if there even had been one, and refused to help her."

"Has she dated since then?"

"I don't think so. At least, she's never mentioned it."

Dom couldn't figure out where this was all heading.

Karla straightened up in her seat and pinned Dom with a look that basically said, *You are being stupid.*

To say Dom paid intense attention from that point forward, was an understatement.

"So. She's never had a man she could depend on. She has no reason whatsoever to trust a man. She's raised a wonderful boy, from what you told me. And she did it all by herself with no one else to help her."

Dom nodded when she stopped speaking. Then she continued with the certainty he was listening and not thinking about sports or cars or anything else.

"Have you asked her to marry you?"

"Not yet." He was starting to squirm now.

"Have you even told her that you loved her?"

"Well, no. At least not out loud."

"What does that mean? Did you write it to her instead?" Karla's voice hardened even more.

"No! You know I'm not a note writer." It was starting to dawn on him that maybe he hadn't been looking at the big picture, but only from his side.

"Well then, how does she know you love her and want to marry her?"

Karla waited for the question to sink in before adding, "Let me guess. You figure she knows all that from what? Your kisses?"

Dom barely moved his head in the affirmative. He knew he was about to be instructed in something he should have known sooner, and he was getting ready for it.

"Didn't the father of her son kiss her, too?"

The question hung there between them before Karla continued.

"And he left her high and dry. So just what experience that she'd had would lead her to believe that she could trust you?

"I'm trustworthy!" Dom was appalled Karla thought he wasn't.

"No! You're not getting this. I'm not saying you are not to be trusted. I know you are! But what have you done to prove to Wren that you are good for your word? What experience has she had that has proven men stick around when she needs them? Why should she blindly trust you?"

He was thinking hard, trying to see what she was saying.

"What do you think she thought when I showed up and you instantly ran out of her place?"

Dom hadn't even seen the situation from that point of view. He knew Karla and he were just friends. Didn't Wren just know he'd never cheat on her?

It slowly started to dawn on him where things kept getting complicated with their relationship.

Karla started to relax when she saw the change happening.

Dom's inner discoveries continued. Didn't Wren think the fundraising calendar was full of half-naked men? Mrs. Abbott had mentioned that in one of their conversations, but Dom had just brushed it aside. He realized he'd been assuming a lot about what Wren thought.

He started to look at things from her standpoint and wasn't happy with what he saw. True, he wasn't deliberately trying to confuse or hurt her, but he came to realize his lack of communicating to her had ended up hurting her anyway. And that made him understand some changes he had to do if he was ever going to win over Wren and her son.

"Why do women have to be so complicated?" Dom's question was sincere and made Karla smile.

"That's just how we're built. Learn to deal with it."

Dom smiled at her. "Thank you. You are really REALLY a good friend, Karla." He reached across her and opened her door. "But I've gotta go right now. I have some stuff I need to handle and the sooner I handle it, the better everyone will feel."

She laughed and hopped out of the truck, shutting the door behind her, then waved through the window as he drove off.

She was happy to be of some help and she really hoped everything worked out for Dom. She headed back to her car, pulled out her phone and called Noah. When he answered she asked if he could call their babysitter; she wanted him all to herself for the rest of the day.

Chapter Thirty-Three

Dom was starting to get discouraged. He'd tried the library, but they weren't there. Then he headed over to the miniature golf place, hoping that was where they'd gone, but they weren't there either.

He swung by the diner where they'd eaten before, but the hostess said they hadn't been in recently.

He decided to call Mrs. Abbott to see if they'd gone to her house.

"Hello?" Mrs. Abbott's high voice usually made Dom smile to himself as he pictured her picking up a curved handset from an old fashioned elegant phone, but not today.

"Hi, Mrs. Abbott. This is Dom."

"I know, Dear. I have caller ID." Sometimes people just tended to treat her like an old lady!

"Oh." Dom wasn't sure where to take that particular bit of information, so he just plowed onward. "I can't find Wren and Caleb. Are they at your place?"

Mrs. Abbott sat up in her chair where she'd been playing Mahjong on her phone when the call came in. "No, they aren't. Were they supposed to be here?"

"No. At least I don't know." He puffed out a breath and continued. "We had a slight misunderstanding and when I got back to her place, they were gone."

She smiled to herself. Good for Wren, not just waiting around for the man. Make him work for it if he really wanted her.

"Well, I just can't help you, Dom." Then she added, "Have to tried asking Wylie's parents? Maybe Caleb is over there."

Dom felt some hope again. "Thank you Mrs. Abbott, I'll do that. Have a nice afternoon."

"Thank you, Dom. You, too." She ended the call and went back to the timed game she'd been playing. She had almost beat her record until she'd taken his call. Now she had to start a new game. Oh well.

Dom and Wylie's dad had exchanged phone numbers when he'd been setting up the seats for the concert, so he called the man.

"Hey, Dom! How's it going?" The man seemed to be perpetually chipper. Dom wished he knew what the secret was.

"Hi. Have you seen Wren and Caleb?"

"Well, sure. She came by here and picked up Wylie for a day at the waterpark. They were going to spend the whole afternoon there."

"Thank you!" Dom's relief was evident in his voice. "I think I'll join them."

"Have fun!"

The call ended and Dom swung by his place to pick up a pair of trunks and a towel before heading over to the park.

"Are you guys hungry yet?" Wren watched Caleb and Wylie dry off from their latest soak in the wave pool.

"Yeah!"

"Me, too!"

"Great! Let's head over to the concession area." Wren realized she was also hungry. Water and sun just seemed to give her a bigger appetite than usual.

The boys had both ordered hot dogs and drinks. Then Wren added her order and waited for the teenager behind the wooden counter to tell her how much it was going to be when she heard Dom's voice.

"And we'll also have another cheeseburger and bottled water." He handed the kid a card and waited.

Wren's heart stopped in her chest as she stood so close to him. He looked down at the top of her head and leaned his shoulder into hers and left it there so they were touching.

She finally looked up at him and he almost melted from the look in them. He could see she wanted to be with him but was hesitant. Now he understood her hesitancy and knew exactly how to make it go away.

"Do you know just how much I love you, Wren?"

The teenager stopped while in the middle of handing the man's card back to him, eyes wide and mouth hanging open. He wasn't sure how to proceed, so just stood frozen as the man declared his love to the woman standing beside him.

"I think I do." Wren's lungs started to relax from the breath she'd been holding.

"Wren, when you're ready, I want to marry you."

Now the teenager didn't know what to do at all. He couldn't keep the man's card, but he didn't think the guy would appreciate him handing the card back right now. No, this was one of those service problems they hadn't trained him for. He wasn't getting paid enough to have to get through this sort of situation.

"Marry me?" Wren's tremulous smile let Dom know he'd just made her happy. And that made him happy.

"Mom!" Caleb's voice came from her other side. "We're starving!"

Well, that broke the romantic spell that had fallen over the concession stand.

Dom reached out and took the card back from the kid and put it in his pocket.

Wren reached over and softly put her hand in Dom's free hand.

The teenager retrieved their orders.

And everyone headed over to one of the empty concrete benches to eat.

The remainder of their day at the park was one of the best days any of them had ever had.

Dom thoroughly enjoyed rubbing sunblock into Wren's back. If he took a little longer than needed, neither of them seemed to mind.

When they rode in one of the two-man canoes at one of the water chute rides, Wren's back up against Dom's chest was almost too much for both of them.

Watching Caleb and Wylie and their hijinks in the water made both adults chuckle.

By the end of the exhausting but blissful day, they were all ready to head home.

Because they had two vehicles, Dom offered to drop off Wylie at his place while Wren and Caleb headed home. He told her he'd join them soon.

"We have some discussing to do." His warm voice told Wren that it was going to be to her liking and she was looking forward to hearing what he had to say.

She and Caleb arrived home. She got him into the shower and then ready for bed.

Just as she'd finished fixing him a snack before his bedtime, she heard a knock at the door.

She rapidly went over, a smile already spreading across her face, and opened it.

Dom was standing there, looking the best she'd ever seen him. He had a slight sunburn from the day's rays. His hair was tousled from just running his fingers through it. He looked tired and contented.

Dom took in everything about Wren in one glance. She was beautiful, standing there in her one-piece suit and beach cover-up. Her bare legs and gorgeous face had gotten some new color that afternoon, which looked amazing to him.

"Dom!" Caleb ran over and hugged him. "I'm so glad you found us! Can you come in?" Dom could see that Caleb was starting to get revved up again, which he knew would make him overtired and a little cranky. But he wanted to stay.

"Tell you what, Dude. If you go to bed when your mom says to without an argument, I'll come in."

"Deal!" Caleb grabbed Dom's hand and pulled him into the apartment.

"Mom fixed be a bedtime snack. Do you want one too?"

Over the child's head, Dom lifted one eyebrow at Wren in a slightly suggestive way. All she did was throw a slight grin in his direction and headed back into the kitchen.

"Peanut butter and jelly or grilled cheese?" Her voice carried out to him in the other room. He glanced down at Caleb who had just nudged him.

"Get the peanut butter and jelly. She always burns the grilled cheese." Caleb's earnest suggestion was so Caleb that Dom had to respond in kind.

"Thank you" he whispered. Then louder he said, "I'll have the peanut butter and jelly, please."

"Good choice." Caleb commended Dom for taking his suggestion, then headed over to his plate and glass of milk he hadn't finished yet.

Dom wandered in behind him just as Wren finished cutting his sandwich into quarters like she usually did for Caleb.

Yep. Dom was definitely going to marry this woman.

The sandwich tasted great.

Wren and Dom were sitting on the couch after Caleb finally fell asleep. Dom was facing her and holding one her hands in his. His thumb gently rubbing back and forth over the back of it.

He'd just finished telling her what he'd come to realize that day while looking for her.

And now it was her turn to talk.

She looked down at her lap and then back up to him.

"You're not the only one who came to some realizations today."

"Really?" Dom hadn't been expecting her statement at all. "What did you come up with?"

"I've built walls around myself. I set up certain standards I had to maintain, even though no one else expected it of me." She shrugged one shoulder. "Well, except maybe my parents. In the end, they told me they'd expected more out of me. They were upset I'd let them down."

"Why? Because you got pregnant?"

"That's what I thought at first, but I still don't think that was the real reason." She looked off to the side and stared at a memory only she could see before continuing. "Up to that point, we'd had a pretty good relationship, I thought." She shook herself out of the doldrums and added, "Well, that was then, not now.

"Now, I have to live with the consequences of any decision I make. And one of the decisions I've decided to change is to give you my trust." She smiled at him. "I don't think you've ever intentionally tried to deceive me in any way. I took it that way because I'd already decided that no man could be trusted. And unfortunately, you bore the brunt of my wrong idea."

"Wow. That's a big change, Wren." He leaned across and gave her a small kiss before leaning back. "I'm proud of you."

Dom's statement hit home for Wren. Yes, she **had** done something pretty great! Deciding to live more openly and honestly had already made her feel better about herself, and others as well.

For once, she could see a good future, not only one where she protected and helped her son but also a future for herself beside the man she loved!

Chapter Thirty-Four

Four Months Later

Wren was sitting behind her new desk at the recently upgraded Largo Bay Library. She was admiring the new ring adorning her left hand.

Dom had asked her to marry him that evening after their day at the waterpark. And she had thrown her arms about his neck and accepted his proposal with no uncertainty whatsoever. The next day when she told Caleb Dom was going to be his father, she was surprised when all she got back from the boy was a small shrug.

"Aren't you happy about that?"

"Oh, sure I am! It's just not a surprise." He continued to mold the piece of clay he was currently shaping into something for his and Wylie's space project.

Wren had sat back in stunned silence. Had she been the only one who had not been certain of a marriage between her and Dom? Apparently, she had been the only one.

Now she felt brighter than she had for years. She could finally look forward to what was ahead.

There was only one thing bothering her. She didn't want to wait to get married. She didn't want a huge ceremony. She didn't want a fancy wedding dress. She didn't want to spend the money on flowers, cake, invitations, and all the other things that usually came with a wedding.

No. She just wanted a quiet joining of their lives, maybe before a justice of the peace, with just her and Dom and Caleb. She frowned for a moment. She had to include Dom's family, too. They would be disappointed if they weren't there.

She'd come to love the McGannon clan and couldn't wait to be one of the family. Especially since she didn't have one of her own anymore.

She hadn't heard once from her parents after that day they'd kicked her out of the house. Not one word. She didn't even know if they still lived at the same house or not. She knew she should just forget about them, however (and it was a huge however) they were Caleb's grandparents.

Yes, Max said he was looking forward to taking his first grandchild, meaning Caleb, to a ballgame or two. And yes, Dom's entire family had instantly claimed her and her son as their own.

But Wren knew it just wasn't the same. It was a problem she tried hard to not put much attention on yet couldn't help doing now that she was getting close to being a married woman. She stopped frowning and made the decision to speak with Dom about her concerns. After all, she had someone she could depend upon.

She also sort of figured he'd be happier with a faster wedding date, too, since he had recently taken to groaning out loud when it was time for him to leave her place. It always made her feel attractive and somewhat powerful.

Mrs. Abbott finished shelving the last cart of books and headed over to Wren's new office. Mrs. Abbott was happy for Mrs. Turner who had decided to permanently move out closer to her new grandchild. And since another one was on the way, she made the move quickly, turning over the library completely into Wren's capable hands.

"All done with the books, Wren!" Mrs. Abbott was heading out early that day from the library. She'd already told Wren about the bocce ball league she joined last week. They were having their first get together tonight and she didn't want to be late.

What she hadn't told Wren was the fact that she was going to be the only female on an all-male team.

She was actually looking forward to the situations she might find herself in, surrounded by older men and her being the only older female.

Maybe she'd even find someone to live out the rest of her life with.

"See you tomorrow!" She headed out the door.

"Have fun!" Wren called after the woman and received a wave over the shoulder in acknowledgement.

Wren turned back to her work and quickly finished up the spreadsheets for the city council. Everything was looking ship shape.

She walked out of her office and crossed to the checkout desk where one of the library's volunteers was sitting.

"Hi, Joyce! How are things going?"

"It's pretty quiet, Ms. Johnson. No one's come in for the past half hour."

"Is there anyone still here?"

"No. No one."

"Okay, I'll take over the desk and you can leave early. Thank you for being here! It means a lot to the Largo Bay Library. Without our volunteers, we would have a difficult time handling everything by ourselves."

Joyce blushed at the compliment. "Thank you, Ms. Johnson. After I graduate from high school, I'm looking forward to studying library science at college. Maybe I could even work here when I have my degree?"

Wren chuckled. "Joyce, you're already working here! But even without a degree, you would be a very capable productive employee anywhere you chose to work. Having said all that, yes, please keep us in mind when you graduate!"

"Thank you!" Joyce grabbed her pack from under the counter and waved goodbye to Wren as she went out the front door.

Wren sat down, knowing it was for only another ten minutes before Dom came to pick her up from work.

The time passed swiftly, especially since Wren was perusing the new book catalogue. She looked up when the grandfather clock that had been donated for their new grand opening chimed six chimes."

And right on the dot, Dom came through the door. After a lengthy kiss that left them both breathless, he helped Wren lock up before heading to his truck. They got inside, but instead of starting up the truck, Dom turned to her and rested a hand on her shoulder.

"I want to ask you something and I want your honest answer, not what you think I might want to hear."

Wren could see the earnestness in his request and told him she would.

"What would you think if we eloped."

Had he been reading her mind? Her smile told him her answer was yes.

She asked, "When?"

"How about right now?"

When he saw her start to pause about all the logistics with Caleb and the library, he added, "I've handled everything already. Caleb is going to stay with Wylie's family and Mrs. Abbott has agreed to run the library while we're gone for a couple of days. There's a justice of the peace already waiting for us just in case you said yes, and I've booked reservations for one of the penthouse suites at the Grand Beach Resort in Ft. Lauderdale.

"So, soon-to-be Mrs. McGannon, what do you think?"

Wren didn't say anything. Instead, she slid over the front seat and wrapped her arms around Dom's neck, giving him the kiss of a lifetime.

When they pulled back for air, he reached behind his seat and pulled out a thin wrapped present and handed it to her.

"Here's your first wedding present!"

Wren could tell by its shape that it was the new firefighter calendar. She braced herself so she wouldn't react badly at seeing a picture of Dom bare chested, probably on the front cover. Now that he was hers, she sure didn't want any other women to get any ideas that he might be available. She just didn't want to have to deal with that sort of thing.

She kept the smile plastered on her face as she unwrapped it. But when she finally got a look at the front cover, the smile left her face. She couldn't believe it. She had been expecting something totally different!

She glanced up at Dom and saw he understood what she was going through.

They both looked down at the calendar and the cover picture of one of the firefighters still in his helmet and turnouts cradling a puppy that was covered with soot.

Wren turned the page. This one was of the fire chief speaking into a walkie-talkie with only the light from a smokey fire illuminating his face which was wreathed with concern.

She looked up at Dom again. "It's not beefcake." Her quiet declaration let him know that he'd been right about her concerns.

"Nope. Not one man chest in the whole thing."

Wren giggled as she flipped through the rest of it, looking for Dom's picture. When she only found him in the group shot on the back cover, her face showed her confusion.

"But I thought you were one of the models."

"No. We pulled names out of a fire hat and luckily my name wasn't one of the ones selected."

"Why did you say *luckily*?" I would have thought you would have liked to be Mr. January or something like that." She was smiling her relief at this point.

"I said luckily because I belong to only one woman, my wife."

Wren sighed and then he added, "Besides, I didn't want to show everyone else up."

She laughed as she launched herself back into his arms for more of his addictive kisses.

At one point, she pulled back with an additional question. "Did you remember to pack a bag for me?"

"Of course. Be forewarned however, there's not much in it except for a swimsuit, a pair of shorts and a cropped top."

"I don't own a cropped top."

"You do now."

The older couple was escorted to Max's office at the police station. He didn't recognize them, but something about them looked familiar.

The woman was clutching an older purse in front of her and the man was guiding her with one of his hands on her elbow. Sort of like he was holding her up.

Max indicated for them to take the two chairs in front of his desk, then sat down after they'd been seated.

The woman still hadn't looked up at him, and the man's attention seemed to be glued to the woman.

Max leaned forward and asked, "What can I do to help you folks."

At his question, the woman started to sniffle. The man pulled out a handkerchief from his pocket and gently handed it to her. She nodded her thanks and proceeded to dab at the tears overflowing from her eyes.

"Ma'am? Are you all right?" Max was starting to grow concerned about them. Were they in some kind of trouble? Had they been robbed or assaulted?

Finally, the man turned his gaze to Max and said, "We're looking for our daughter."

When he said that, the woman choked out a sob.

Max pulled out a form from his file cabinet and started to fill it in.

"Okay. First, Sir, what is your name please?"

"Wayne Johnson and this is my wife, Raelynn."

Max entered their names on the form.

"And your daughter's name, please?"

"Wren Johnson. Her name is Wren, like the bird."

Max stopped writing and slowly set down his pencil. He sat back in his chair and brought his fingertips together in front of his mouth.

"Mr. and Mrs. Johnson. There is something I need to tell you."

THE END

Author Request

If you liked this book, please leave a review on either Amazon or Goodreads!
Good reviews are the bread and butter of life for indie authors!

Sneak Peek!

FINDING FOREVER: BOOK 5 IN THE LARGO BAY SERIES

"I now pronounce you husband and wife. You may kiss the bride." The justice of the peace couldn't have sounded more pleased. In fact, you would think he'd brought the couple together himself.

Dom release Wren's hand that he'd been holding during the ceremony and cupped both sides of her beautiful face.

He leaned down and gave her the most gentle, most loving, most emotion filled kiss he could.

Then, he wrapped both arms around her and bent her over backwards for a completely enthusiastic ravaging of her mouth. When he finally brought her back upright all she could do was hang onto his arm so she didn't melt to the ground.

Wow! The man could sure kiss!

The officiant laughed at the grins on both their faces before congratulating them, then having them both sign the bottom of the license. He also had them sign his own version of an old fashioned marriage certificate, which Wren thought had probably been his wife's idea.

He handed the original copy to his wife who was always his witness for marriages, and who always cried at each and every one of them as though they were her own.

"The usual number of copies, Sweetheart."

She hurried into the office next door and Dom and Wren could hear the photocopier doing its thing.

They exchanged small talk with the man until his wife returned with their copies in an envelope.

"Be sure to take the original to the County Clerk to get your marriage recorded. They will issue your official marriage certificate."

He shook Dom's hand and his wife gave Wren a tiny hug.

Then the blissfully happy, newly wedded couple was back in Dom's truck and heading to the hotel for their wedding night.

"Dom? Give me a call back when you get this, okay?" Max left a second message for his son, hoping he would hear from him sooner rather than later. He was uncomfortable not being able to reach either Wren or Dom. It wasn't like them to not pick up or at least text back.

He left his office and went back down the hall to the small waiting area at the police station. Mr. and Mrs. Johnson were sitting in two of the chairs just staring into space.

They'd never thought they would ever be so close to finding their little girl. Years ago, they'd both come to realize that they'd made a terrible mistake by believing the young man who had come by their house just hours before their own daughter came home to tell them she was expecting.

When Wren had tried to explain to them about Stanley and what had happened, they were blinded by the lies he'd told them. They hated the fact that they'd believed him instead of their own daughter. They'd accused her viciously of sleeping around with a number of men. When Stanley told them he wasn't even sure if the child was his, they'd unfortunately fallen for it.

And they'd paid for the horrible actions they'd committed on that day they'd kicked her out. For almost a decade now, they'd prayed every single day to find her and ask for her forgiveness.

They were finally going to be able to see their daughter and grandchild after years and years of searching. If it hadn't been for an anonymous letter sent to them, they wouldn't have ever known to go to Florida to find her.

They would forever be grateful for that person's note.

"Mr. and Mrs. Johnson?" They both turned their eyes up to where Max was standing in the doorway. "I haven't been able to reach either my son or your daughter yet, but I'll keep trying. In the meantime, I think you should probably go get a room at one of Largo Bay's hotels. If you want, I could call around for you."

Mr. Johnson was the first to respond. He stood up and spoke to his wife. "Raelynn, I think the man is right. Let's go find a place to stay for now."

She nodded in agreement and gathered her purse before getting to her feet.

"You don't think she's hurt, do you?" The woman's chin trembled. It might have been from fear for her daughter's safety, but Max would have placed money on the idea she hadn't eaten or slept for days now.

"No, Ma'am. They're probably at a concert or something like that. I'm sure I'll hear back from them within a few hours. I'll contact you as soon as I do."

The Johnson's both nodded and headed back out to their car. It wasn't until they'd driven out of the parking lot that they'd forgotten to get the name of a good hotel for them to stay at.

Max hadn't forgotten though, and called the Manager at one of the local five star facilities and asked if they could offer a room for a couple of days at a lowered price. Max didn't think the Johnson's had a lot of money. The Manager agreed and booked the room.

Then Max texted the couple, letting them know the address and who to ask for when they got there.

Now, he had to track down his son.

He had no idea what had become of Dom and worry was starting to nibble around the edges of his mind.

This was exactly what he didn't need tonight.

Tonight, he was taking a woman out to dinner and he'd been engulfed all day with guilt, trepidation, and excitement each taking center stage for a few moments before the next one took its place.

He hadn't told any of his kids because he didn't know what to say.

If it turned out he and Marlene really got along, he prayed his children would like and accept her, but not as a mother replacement. No, that was not it. No one would ever be able to replace Luz.

He just didn't want to live the rest of his life alone.

It had been almost a year since she'd died.

It had been almost two years since she'd been diagnosed.

He'd had two years to grieve for her and was finally now seeing a little light enter the darkness he'd been surrounded with for over twenty-four months.

Max truly hoped his children would be happy he was finally starting to live again.

Get your copy of Finding Forever

Also by Pat Adeff

Welcome to the *Second Chances DO Happen* Series!

Book 1: Take Another Chance
Book 2: Mahi-Mahi Matrimony
Book 3: The Romance Writer and the Geek
Book 4: To Heal A Heart
Book 5: In His Arms
Book 6: A Christmas Kiss

I would love it if you'd go to my website and join my newsletter at www.patadeff.com to learn about upcoming releases!
Also, if you liked this book, please leave a review! Good reviews are the bread and butter of life for an indie author!
If you didn't like something about this book, contact me at www.patadeff.com and let me know why.
I want to give readers wonderful stories and am always looking for ways to do just that.

Made in the USA
Coppell, TX
10 October 2025